For Judy —

Enjoy!

Bill Robinson

# *Bottom Pig*

***a novel in three stories***

ABOUT THE AUTHOR . . .

WILLIAM ROBINSON was born in Raleigh, North Carolina. He attended Morehouse College, Howard University, the University of Paris, and LeMoyne-Owen College, and was graduated from Olivet College and New York University. After working one year toward a doctorate, he went to Yaddo, and to France with a John Hay Whitney Foundation Opportunity Fellowship in Writing. He has since studied at the Universidad Católica in Ponce, Puerto Rico, and he has worked at writing, editing, and public relations in Arizona, Mexico, New York, and New Jersey.

# BOTTOM PIG

*a novel in three stories*

*by William Robinson*

When black and white are grey, there is no middle ground.

—Gerd Stern

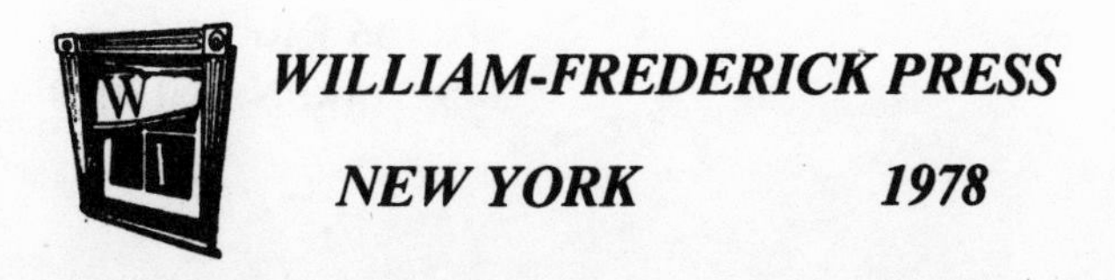

*WILLIAM-FREDERICK PRESS*

*NEW YORK* *1978*

Manufactured in the United States of America


"Segregation" is based on *The Squad,* A Comedy in Three Acts, Copyright © 1977 and 1950 by William Albert Robinson, Jr. "Integration" is based on "El de las 7.10 a París," serialized in *TRENTO,* Periódico del Seminario de Morelia, Michoacán, México, October and December 1960, Copyright © 1960 by Guillermo Robinson S., and on *Death of the Blue Canary,* a Play in Two Acts, Copyright © 1965 by David Rankin. William Robinson, Guillermo Robinson S., and David Rankin are names by which William Albert Robinson, Jr. is also known.

Grateful acknowledgment is made to Harvard University Press for the use of the song of the Rebel Soldier, from John Harrington Cox, *Folk-Songs of the South,* 1925, variant versions of which date from 1862.



Library of Congress Catalog Card Number: 77-88615
International Standard Book Number: 0-87164-045-7
First edition, 1978

William-Frederick Press
55 East 86 Street
New York, N.Y. 10028

also by William Robinson

*Beloved Outcaste*

(a screenplay based on the biography
*Bishop Healy: Beloved Outcaste*
by Albert S. Foley, S.J.)

for

\+ Jonathan

# *Contents*


| | |
|---|---|
| **PREFACE** | 1 |
| *SEGREGATION* | 3 |
| *DESEGREGATION* | 45 |
| *INTEGRATION* | 100 |

# *Bottom Pig*

***a novel in three stories***

---

# *Preface*

THE HERO as madman, or madwoman, has dwelled in the novel since its inception, as in some of the better examples—Cervantes, Dostoevski, Flaubert. Why so, is not a matter controlled by the authors—as here, segregation is like a stone thrown, carrying within itself the curve of its flight. Those carried along by the adventure, as though within the projectile—in this case, an army truck, an ambulance, and a weapons-carrier—presume that man has believed and will always believe the same things *they* do, which is a vanity. He who would confront that vanity is as someone born to live in another time, yet drawn into the present, there to risk becoming, like Hamlet, one for whom the immediate concern diverts hope for the day when there will be no longer the need to be mad. José Ortega y Gasset has written, "It is true that Don Quixote is not rational. But the problem is not solved by declaring Don Quixote insane. What in him is abnormal, has been and will continue to be normal in humanity." This would explain it, if it were blessedly true that all of humanity were appropriately mad, but so far it has been rare to the point of becoming confused with a kind of vaunted and lonely individualism. To the contrary, it is a position in one sense even more lonely, in another, not lonely at all, as in our own time, among the few, Daisetz T. Suzuki and Fr. Pierre Teilhard de Chardin,

S.J.—to side with the self-conscious universe, against unself-conscious man.

Absolve the typesetter for my understanding that street language intends by *black* exactly what is intended by *white,* lower case, as street people are without the intellectual's failures to demand the absolute.

With much gratitude, I wish to acknowledge my indebtedness to the John Hay Whitney Foundation, to Yaddo, and for their advice and assistance, to Elsie Van Ness, Joseph Dexter Bennett, W. H. Auden, Louise Bogan, James F. Mathias, Malcolm Cowley, Cyrilly Abels, Alvin Levin, and John Howard Griffin.

WILLIAM ROBINSON

# *Segregation*

# *I*

INTEGRATION—there was no such word. There was "desegregation," and even that hadn't yet been tried by the Army by edict. When it was, there was nothing more simply done—like black and white chess pieces consecutively moved into each other's squares. But for *integration* there is more within a man than can be moved by edict. The old convictions about how the game is played must be erased. For this the pieces must be scattered from the board, cast into some outer darkness where it is impossible to tell black from white, and there, in that darkness, employed in a game.

Not many have played such a game and lived—Jonah, Jason, and Dostoevski. Among the few, and not the last, Paul Ross—Private Paul Ross, with the 49th Salvage, QMC, in France—one of some two hundred black pawns not yet moved consecutively into white men's squares. Ross was their baby-shit-colored nigger, and therefore a hard man to desegregate, perhaps the hardest of all. However unprepared, as with the prophets before him like Jonah, Jason, and Dostoevski, he made it home, bringing the word.

It all began for him the night before Halloween, 1944, all of life having taken on the proportions of that feast, as the unities of place and time.

DEAD to the world, his eyes slept, but he watched with his flesh, and recorded the pulse of the night. Some fifty yards away a prickle of small arms fire drummed into loose earth, but his flesh had forgotten that this was a tent, and remembered the hole in the ground, the last place he slept. There was no need to wake up at small arms fire when you slept in a hole in the ground.

This was the front yard of a chateau, inside a ragged storage tent, with a wooden platform two feet high and dry in the area between the poles, and a rose bush just inside the tent door. On the platform, six men slept in zippered bags with their rifles and packs thrown in a heap between them, and near the rose bush a rusted sheet metal stove waited for its pipe to be brought in from whichever truck where it was misplaced when they evacuated the last area.

Twice in the night he had felt the thump of bombs diving through the earth and exploding up again, but they fell too far away for him to awaken. And as he dreamed, his fingernails printed into his palms and he craned up inside the sleeping bag, until he let himself back down into the sea of things his mind contained. . . .

"You don't use that service club," a voice said from behind him, thick with anger. "You don't use that service club, that's for colored soldiers."

He felt a rifle dig into his back, and the voice said to him, "Let's me and you walk out in these woods."

So he walked, with his hands in the air, picking his way in the dark. He was not afraid. When you're afraid, you are not altogether convinced of what is going to happen, but he was convinced. There was a glow of light and faint music coming from the service club. When he could no longer hear that music, he would know they had gone far enough for no one to hear the rifle.

The music faded into the noise of their feet on dead

leaves. Without being told, he stopped and stood waiting to hear the explosion behind him. The voice asked him, "How come you don't say nothing?" The muzzle of the rifle began to tremble against his back. *"Soldier!"* the voice screamed at him. *"What's the matter with you, soldier! How come you don't say nothing!"*

A light moved across his face, and he woke up.

"Lay on down, Ross, don't nobody want you," and the light moved on, finding the face of each man in the tent, until it found Gary.

Gary opened his eyes, "Nigger, get that flashlight out of my face."

"Don't call me no nigger, how you know I ain't the Lieutenant?"

Gary rose up in his sleeping bag and squinted at the light, "Nigger, you turn that thing off before I jump up from here and stick it down your mouth!"

The flashlight went out.

In the dark, Gary said, "That white man know better than to come in here. What the hell you want?"

"Finley come in yet?"

"How I'm spose to know?"

"He sleep in here."

"That's his business."

"All right, old smart nigger, what I'm spose to cook?"

"You couldn't cook nothing if he brought it in here, you big greasy hog."

"I bet Ernestine don't say that."

"Motherfucker, *turn* that flashlight on!"

"All right, I'll go see The Man and find out how come Finley ain't in here."

"You better go on back in that chateau while you can still make it."

The mess sergeant fumbled around in the dark until he found the door of the tent. "It don't hurt me none if Finley don't come in. I done ate mines."

Gary thrashed around in his sleeping bag, trying to go back to sleep. "Big greasy South Ca'lina hog, all the time running to that cracker. . . ."

And Ross drifted under the prow of a word, a hard, jagged word that parted the waters and stood high against him: *cracker* . . . *Cracker* . . . CRACKER. . . .

Ross was just five years old and he ran out on the front porch into the summer sun and banged the screen door against the swarm of flies struggling to go the other way. In the street below, the big children were running and he wanted to run and throw rocks at the boy in front, the way they were doing. He called to them, "What you doing?"

"We're chasing a cracker."

Ross tried to see how you play that. The boy in front was crying against a hedge, trying to get his breath, while the rest took their time picking up rocks.

Ross wanted to do it, too. He came down the front steps, but they wouldn't let him play.

"You can't chase crackers."

"Yes, I can," he said.

"Naw, you can't. You'd just mess it up—way down the street children a-think *you* the cracker."

While they were talking, the white boy ran silently to the other side of the street, but a shout went up, "Yon he come! Yon he come! Head him back the other way!"

Ross stood screwing up his face to cry; then he ran back into the house, straight to the kitchen. They were still there, on the kitchen table, a whole boxful, a whole box of crackers. . . .

The prickly sting of the sound was near this time, small arms fire. It was shattering glass and the pieces fell. . . .

You don't have to wake up in a foxhole, at least not in this company, the 49th Salvage, because it's got to be just somebody shooting to be shooting, acting a fool. . . . The broken windshield fell on the floor of the car, and for a moment he stared at the chrome figure of a running dog on the radiator cap as though he had never seen it before. Ross threw open the door and slid from under the steering wheel and ran. . . . He ran. . . .

He was not sure how to dream this, because he had

never seen a race riot. He ran silently to the other side of the street as a shout went up, "Yon he come! Yon he come! Head him back the other way!"

Ross tried the screen door but it was locked firm as a wall, and ripping open with a row of holes above his head. In the movies, if the row of holes is above the guy's head, then you know he's not getting shot. They were shooting a machine gun at Ross from the hotel on the other side of the street. He turned to face the hotel and watch it shoot at him. In the movies, if you turn around and watch people shoot at you, that means they can't hit you. Then suddenly the screen door came open, and he crawled inside. No one was there. He dragged himself on, clinging to furniture as he went. Something in a pot was smoking up the stove in the kitchen, and he turned off the gas. His mother never did figure out how that gas got turned off. Out the back door, he looked up through the laundry floating from the back porches, one above the other, and he began to run up, up, flight after flight of wooden steps, and across porch after porch, until he reached the roof.

He dropped flat and crawled to the front of the house and looked down into the street. His car was still there where he left it among the others. The door hung open. Someone was still shooting from the second story window of the hotel into his front porch.

A long black car rolled in around the corner of the street, with small round holes at the bottom of dents in its roof. It rolled on slowly, machine-gunning the hotel window. Then it stopped and police got out. They walked toward the hotel; then they all fell down. There were a lot of them now, men lying in the street. Some were dead, some afraid to move.

Paul Ross was sure he knew the man in the hotel window. It was Collins. He owned the hotel. He was standing in the window with a machine gun, looking and waiting. Paul yelled from the roof without showing himself, "Collins! It's me! Ross!"

Collins leveled his machine gun at Paul's roof, then

lowered it. Paul yelled again, "Up here!" and he waved.

Collins waved back, "Don't worry, I know you."

Ross watched a grenade as it spun upward from the far corner of the street, over all the parked cars, toward Collins. It exploded in the hotel window; then Collins was down, lying on the sidewalk. His right arm flapped back and forth gripping the trigger, until his machine gun was empty. But now Ross could not go on with the dream, not with Collins dead. "Yes, I can," he said aloud in his sleep.

"Naw, you can't," Collins told him, but his tone of voice was friendly. "It's because you don't use that service club, fellow, so why don't you just go do something else."

There was the soft thump, thump of bombs, again, and he swept out the car and polished it, and the windows were so clean that he almost broke his watch putting his hand out to make a turn when they drove away from the dance. It was just beginning to rain, thump, thump, and the radio was on low.

They parked and sat chilling in the autumn night, listening to dance music on the car radio and the drops of rain pelting the car. Tillie sat curled up under his arm, with her shoes off. Her party dress billowed all over the seat, and her corsage of talisman roses nestled under his chin. Tillie had beautiful eyes, larger than most people's, and so bright in the night, as though she was just eyes and nothing else, because her skin was so dark. But smoke was coming right out of her hair.

"Honey, you shouldn't do that to your hair. I don't care what anybody says," he told her, but Tillie was already gone, and the scent of talisman roses, all gone. He was unable to breathe and he choked on each inward breath. His hands plunged out of the sleeping bag to find his gas mask. He tore the sack open, and pulled the mask down over his face. As he sat breathing deeply, he tested the cannister and the connecting rubber hose. The fogged eyepieces began to clear, and Ross could see a fire licking out of the sheet metal stove, and Gary, with an ax, just inside the door of the tent, cutting down a rose bush.

Ross took off his gas mask and put it away. It had been Gary. Gary had dropped a match in on wet wood and gasoline, and the explosion had blown soot out of the stove. But he had found their stovepipe.

Ross was thinking he had taken Tillie to a dance. Why in the hell would he think that? He had never taken Tillie to any dance, and never would, not the way she acted, and he was not in his foxhole, because it was full up with water, now. This was not even where they were on the Meuse River. This was someplace else. He had heard somebody say where they were, last night when they drove in, in all that rain. They were right up beside another river, and a big chateau.

Ross brought an arm out of his sleeping bag and licked his fingers to clear the corners of his eyes, and scrub his teeth on the collar of his shirt. It was icy cold outside the sleeping bag. Near his face the sleeping bag was frozen and stiff from his breath.

With his knees he unwound the sleeping bag until the zipper was in front of him and running evenly along his body toward his feet. Then he reached out and lifted the side of the tent to let in light. The thin ice cracked over a sag, and cold water ran down over his hand. He rubbed the water into the sockets of his eyes and up his nose, and dried his freezing fingers on the sleeping bag. He ran his hand down his rifle to make sure it was there, and zipped himself up in his bag, again.

Outside the tent there was the distant mutter of a light artillery barrage and someone beating a spoon clean on the edge of a garbage can. Ross remembered his feet, and he smiled. He had trench foot, at least they all thought he did, and today—this very day—he was supposed to leave the company and get taken to a hospital. It was like a dream, leaving the company.

He looked at the others sleeping on the wooden platform with him—Snow, with his face inside his sleeping bag, only pretending he was asleep because he was breaking wind. And Roscoe, he was asleep, grinding his teeth. And

Gary's empty bag where he sat on it building the fire. And Skin, old Skin, blowing steam and ice into his beard. And the kid, Theophilus, propped up against the pile of packs and rifles.

As a matter of fact, he was supposed to be leaving the company as soon as Finley came back with the truck. It was like some kind of a children's story to be leaving the company. It was like he had dreamed it.

Outside, Gary turned on the motor in the No. 1 trailer, the power generator, and Ross could hear the day shift coming down out of the chateau to go to work, and Sergeant Johnston. "Hup, two, three, four— How come you all can't do right? Hup, two, three, for Jesus *knows* I don't want to be out here this time in the morning. Hup, two, three, halt. Halt, damn it! Bring your ass back here!"

Ross thought he could hear Finley and raised the side of the tent to see. Williams, the mess sergeant, was watching the road from the door of the chateau, and Hughes, the second cook, ran out beside him. They could hear it, good and loud, but the road was empty. Then Williams pointed into the sky, "Yon he come! Yon he come!" He grabbed his apron and ran down the steps, right past the trailers and tents, going for the woods. A buzz bomb came in low over the chateau and kept going.

Gary started laughing and hollered down from where he was up on a ladder, stringing electric cable to a tree. "Run, nigger! You big greasy South Ca'lina hog! I hope you run right under it!"

Williams was walking back, winded. He stopped and leaned on a trailer, looking at Gary in the tree. "Aw, nigger, you shut up."

"Don't be calling me no nigger, you white-mouth South Ca'lina hog!"

Williams straightened up and continued walking back toward the kitchen. "If Finley don't bring his ass on in here, I will go tell The Man."

"Go head on! Go head on! White-mouth to The Man. That won't get Finley in here no quicker!"

Williams turned around. "You put me in mind of a little monkey swinging around in that tree, signifying on me. You better look at what you're doing! You know you never been up that high on Mr. Newdy's farm!"

Gary climbed down the tree and pulled the cable and ladder along with him, and went up to hook into the power connections on the wall of the chateau. "Don't be telling me about a Mr. Newdy. You wasn't no better, in the street peddling swamp seed and gater tail. All you know how to do is wake up in the morning and put your big fat feet up to a big hot stove, and eat."

Williams snapped back, "You don't be telling the Mess Sergeant when he eat!"

"—A man get up this early in the morning just to eat. You don't work but every other day."

"What you talking bout—I got two hundred mens to feed. A hundred all day and a hundred all night. I ain't spose to work but every other day."

Gary ran the cable around the connection and pulled angrily, making the tree bend behind him. "Ain't but one of me, out here every day *and* every night. A man get up this early in the morning just to—" He yanked on the cable, "*—eat!*"

Williams yelled up at him, "I bet that ain't what Ernestine get up this early in the morning to do!"

Gary let the wire go slack. "I done told you, now! I don't play that! You don't know my wife! You mens in the kitchen ain't spose to be reading everybody's service record!"

Williams grinned and leaned over to his second cook, standing in the kitchen door. "Hey, Hughes, what you reckon Ernestine be doing this time in the morning?"

Hughes pretended he had to study about it awhile; then he smiled. "I reckon she be in the bed screaming and creaming!"

The two of them laughed and went back in their kitchen.

# II

THE GROUND shook as the buzz bomb exploded deep in the woods. Hearing the bang, Ross pulled the long zipper on his sleeping bag and greeted himself, "Well, happy Halloween," but that sounded more like the Fourth of July. It didn't make any more difference what day it was, or did it?

Yes, it did, because he could go to the hospital as soon as Finley showed up with the truck, so Ross sat buttoning the mud-spattered army shirt and trousers he had slept in.

Sitting in his sleeping bag, buttoning his uniform, always reminded him of when he was a Boy Scout, and made him angry. When he was eight years old, there were only the white Scouts, so his parents and a group of other parents went downtown to the department store and bought a lot of copies of the *Wolf Cub Scout Book,* and told the children to learn it, to be ready for when the parents got through desegregating the Scouts. Their parents never did get through, until Ross was too old. He worked on that one book for four years, until he had practically memorized it.

As he sat buttoning, he recited, "Are you eight years old? If you are you may join the Cub Scouts. First you become a Bobcat. This means you are a new Cub Scout."

His father said, "Say the Law of the Pack. Tell what it means."

Ross said, "The Cub Scout follows Akela."

His father said, "Now tell what Webelos means."

Ross said, "Fuck a Webelos," and reached deep in his sleeping bag for a bottle of wine. The wine was warm, what was left of it, and he drank it all.

When he was twelve years old, the parents had worked it out that he could be an official Boy Scout, but "so as not to possibly disgrace the uniform," he would have to complete everything to be a First Class Scout before his parents could buy his uniform. Also it got fixed so it wouldn't be any more niggers going into department stores buying things they weren't supposed to have. But by the time he had completed everything to be a Second Class Scout, the rule had been changed so a Second Class Scout could have a uniform. And by the time he was a First Class Scout, even a Tenderfoot could wear the uniform, but a black Scout still couldn't have merit badges, so Ross became a Red Cross lifeguard.

When they were kids they would have been whipped if they had asked why their parents even cared whether they could be Scouts—none of their parents had ever been Scouts. And what in hell was there to it? By the time Ross was twelve years old he could do anything with a rifle that he could do now. They all could. They could take a rifle out in the woods and knock all the pecans out of a tree, and shoot catfish under water, which wasn't easy to do. And in high school he had slept with a police thirty-eight under his pillow, and so had his mother, because his father traveled, and they didn't get them from the police. In the South, black people had guns and knew how to use them, and white people knew what they'd be going up against if they started anything. And there were white men that got shot, even if nobody was supposed to know how it happened. For that matter, what was he doing still alive, yes, himself, still walking around—the naked question jumped at him out of the night's dreams as though Ross had been fighting the war. In combat, finding oneself still alive can become something beyond the simple arithmetic of who you were before, but for Ross the question had nothing to do with the war. He should have been dead before he came overseas.

*He had been taken out to be shot.* Is that what happened? He couldn't remember. He couldn't remember why he hadn't put up a struggle. And in the cold light of morning, all he could remember was that there had been a lynching right on the army post, just before he was drafted. It had been one of the men in his own outfit, Post Cadre, Section II. Ross had been told how they found him, mutilated and hanging from a tree over the black, separate-but-equal swimming pool, behind the black service club. What the

Army did about it was to fill in the swimming pool with dirt, and grow grass over it, and build another black swimming pool beside it.

Post Cadre, *Section II,* was the army way of saying you were black. The men in Section II were black army regulars, all nearly illiterate, except for a few draftees, so nothing else happened, at least not for a while. Things went on as usual. As a college student, Ross was quickly assigned as a clerk at post headquarters, where he seldom saw anyone from his cadre, unless they had business with the records section. Ross usually stayed around the office in the evening, to type letters, and read books from school. He had been told nobody had the time to give him basic training. And the last thing every night, he would walk past the new swimming pool to the service club, to have a beer before going to bed.

From post headquarters, taking a short cut through the woods, Ross would pass an isolated barracks that nearly always stood dark and empty when he went by. It was living quarters for civilians, black women who worked in white homes of majors and colonels living with their families on the post.

While Ross was away on a three-day pass, one night some white paratroopers invaded that barracks. The incident was swept under the rug, and the post commander mounted a twenty-four hour guard on that barracks, using men from Post Cadre, Section II.

When Ross came back from his three-day pass, he had just enough time to go get a beer at the service club before going to bed, but on his way through the woods he was halted and told to put his hands in the air. He felt the muzzle of a rifle in his back and the guard asked him, "Where in the hell do you think you're going?"

"I'm going to the service club to get a beer," Ross answered.

The muzzle of the rifle began to tremble against his back. "Don't lie to me! You don't use that service club—that's for *colored* soldiers!" The rifle moved away from Ross and he heard the bolt being opened. Black soldiers on guard duty weren't allowed to have a loaded rifle. When the bolt closed again, Ross knew it was loaded. The men in his cadre all carried a stolen round of rifle ammunition somewhere in a pocket. You would see them in the service club when somebody pulled out a handful of change to pay for a beer.

The rifle was held firmly at his back now, and the guard said, "Let's me and you walk out in these woods."

The situation was clear enough, without his having to know what had happened on the post while he was away —he was going to be shot. He had been mistaken for white, and by a member of his own cadre. Like the man holding the rifle, Ross hated white people. But without the appearance of a black man, and in order to be accepted as black, his hatred was more malignant. Now that hatred had been turned upon him, and was to cost him his life.

Walking into the woods in the outer darkness, he was robbed rather than killed—robbed of all conviction about his hatred for white people, not for long, minutes perhaps, but long enough for him never to be entirely sure about that again, nor about many things he still could not dare to question. But those few minutes would lengthen as the months went by, and extend their effect.

With his hands in the air, he had walked to his death; yet that had not been the appearance he gave. To the man holding the rifle, Ross had seemed entirely unconcerned about saving his life. He kept walking without being told to go, and he was actually leading the way. The impression was one of bravery, of a willingness to die that was inhuman. The soldier had tried to speak to Ross but could not get his attention, even when he started screaming at him. He was armed with a loaded rifle, but he was becoming completely terrified by this man he had been willing to kill.

It was when Ross finally stopped walking and stood still and quiet, with his hands in the air, that the whole point of killing him was lost completely. The rifle fell out of the guard's hands, and he asked if Ross was in some kind of invasion-trained outfit on drugs.

It was now a whole year since that happened. Why had he never thought of it before? Remembering it now, Ross was unable to feel what it had been like, merely able to recite some details, and the details he had recited were fading. Had somebody actually put a rifle to his back and walked him into the woods? And why had he dreamed about Tillie? It was years since they had said five words to each other. You can go crazy in a war. . . .

"The Cub Scout follows Akela," he said aloud to the sleeping men around him, and finished buttoning his clothes, then pulled his feet out of the sleeping bag. They hurt. He put on his shoes without lacing them, hung his rifle over his shoulder, picked up his steel helmet, and with some effort walked out of the tent to look at the chateau. His first steps were painful. After that, his feet were just numb, as though they weren't really there.

He had tried a number of things to keep his feet from getting worse, slapping them, rubbing them with cognac, heating his shoes on the exhaust pipe of a truck, and going barefoot for short periods to excite circulation. There had been no chance to stay off them entirely. The company had been too busy pulling itself out of the river that was flooding the last area. They had worked nearly all night towing the trailers that now stood lined up on the left of his tent, and on the right three more tents stood cold and empty, their camouflage a network of frozen rain. It was time to unweave the green strips from the nets and use more orange and red—the trees had turned. But it was all they'd had time to do, getting on dry ground.

Where they were before was on the Meuse River, just a creek two feet wide when they got there. Then it started to rain and snow. The river came up through the ground into foxholes and pup tents, until they were hip deep in water, trying to lead the trailers between foxholes, up to the highway. Wet and frozen to each other on top of the equipment boxes, they had moved up in convoy, stopping and turning where bridges were washed away.

Ross hobbled along, looking inside each empty tent—rose bushes. And facing the tents on the other side of the driveway, an old French servant and his wife sat at breakfast behind polished windows. They nodded to him with broad smiles and went on talking in the warmth behind the windowpanes. In windows above them, dried beans hung in their pods over cases of army equipment, Sergeant Neal's quarters, and the company supply room.

This end of the chateau had only one story and an attic, but the rest went up four floors, with a tower at the other end, out over the river. It was all made of cement, dyed to look like old stone. Just beyond the servants, there was a large rounded gateway to give the appearance of a stable, and inside were washtubs built into the wall, and drums of army diesel oil, and cans of gasoline. As Ross passed the kitchen stairway, Sergeant Williams came out and sat on the steps.

"Ross, your feet hurt you?"

Ross nodded that they did.

"Don't look like it's going to be nothing but them K rations if Finley don't come in here, and buzz bombs keep a-coming over. You reckon it be any Germans down in that basement?"

"Might be a few dead ones," Ross said.

"Don't start no foolishness like that with me. Where you reckon Finley went?"

"I'd like to know," Ross said, "because I need the truck."

"And five more white people to feed," Williams said.

"Five?"

"It's three on the top floor, and two more in that part under Neal. I ain't going to feed them. They got no business living with soldiers."

"It's their house," Ross said.

"I don't give a damn whose house it is," Williams said. "They may look like you, but they sure don't look like me—I ain't going to feed them."

Williams went back to his stove, and Ross walked on

toward the river.

By the time Ross and his squad had a chance to think about where they were going to sleep, they were told that the chateau was already full, so they moved into a storage tent, together, the way they had lived when the company was in pup tents.

Ross went out the chateau gate, crossed the road, and climbed a hill to where someone had dug a latrine. Hughes, the second cook, was there buttoning his pants, kicking loose earth behind him into the toilet pit. And there was a goat, shot a number of times in the side, and cold in its own blood.

"Is that for us to eat?" Ross asked him.

"*You* might eat something like that," Hughes told him, "but wouldn't nobody else in this company eat something like that." Hughes blew his nose between his fingers at the dead goat, and went back down the hill. Ross was sure he would not wash his hands, but there was no food either.

Ross stood urinating while he looked up the long narrow road, and at the chateau before him. He would have liked to see Finley coming down the road. Williams was standing on the kitchen steps wringing steam out of hot dish towels, and Gary was astride the ridge pole of their tent, hammering in an electric insulator. Gary poked a cable down the opening for the stovepipe, and someone below pulled it in. Sergeant Neal was assembling two antiaircraft machine guns, and some of the men were sitting on the kitchen steps, scrubbing out mess kits with mud and sand, and dipping them in cans of hot water—hot soapy water, hot sterilizer, and hot rinse water. Some stood pressed against each other in a queue, waiting for Williams to say the word for them to walk through the kitchen and out again.

Everybody knew Williams wasn't anywhere near ready to say the word, but this was the company's game, three times a day, and with nothing better to do it could be played for as long as an hour. The men in the front of the chow line would press their weight backward against the rest, who leaned forward, sealing the line against men trying to break in, like a great laughing centipede that menaced outsiders with flailing mess kits. The game was for outsiders to get past the mess kits, ram one leg through the line, get in a sitting position on the back and chest of two men pressed together, and settle slowly to the ground between them.

While Ross watched, a slim West Indian they called "The Spider" was forced out of his position against the kitchen door at the head of the line. The game on Spider was to make him talk, especially when he was angry. The men shouted for him to go to the end of the line, but he knotted his bony fist down near his knees and squared off at the man who had taken his place, "I'm most bleed your gums, Mr. Son-of-a-bitch."

The men in the line alternated between roars of laughter and shushing each other so they could all hear The Spider.

Ross walked across the road and back toward the chateau. He felt it was his fault they were picking on Spider. Just as they were going overseas, when Ross was transferred to the 49th Salvage, they had tried to start a game on him as the baby-shit-colored nigger. When he wouldn't get in it, an ex-boxer called "Old Doodoo" threw a punch at Ross. It happened in the mess hall with everyone looking. Ross had a plate in his hands, going back for seconds. Old Doodoo put his foot out to trip him but his timing was off, and Ross stepped on his ankle. As Ross turned around he could see the fist coming. There was an explosion against his jaw. Standing facing the company, still with the plate in his hands, he saw a blurred vision of Old Doodoo on the floor, writhing in pain, and the entire company rising to its feet in amazement.

Ross had been nearly knocked cold without going down. Not until he dropped the plate did his balance shift stiffly backward. By then, Sergeant Williams had walked up behind him, and Ross came out of it leaning on Williams. Old Doodoo was given a fast medical discharge with a permanently disabled hand. Nobody in the 49th Salvage ever bothered Ross from that time on, and the new replacement brought in for Old Doodoo was Spider Jones.

As Ross walked past the chow line, Spider now had his foot caught between a man's hip and the kitchen door. The man was saying, "Spider, you hadn't ought to talk to me like that. Ain't I'm your buddy?" The men laughed as Spider tried to ram his way back in next to the kitchen door.

"I done told you, Spider, you my buddy. If I let you in, I'll have to let all my buddies in."

Sergeant Johnston, the day-shift sergeant, was in charge of the chow line, and stood eating from a K-ration can of scrambled eggs. "Go head on to the end of the line," he told Spider, "I seen you when you broke in, in the first place."

Spider waved his mess kit furiously in the air. "Sergeant, how I'm bust in the line when I'm in front?"

"Go head on, now, Spider. Do like I told you to do."

Spider started down the kitchen steps toward the end of the line while the men laughed and yelled and pressed the line tight as he walked past, waving mess kits and rifles in his face. Somewhere down the line, he was poked in the behind with a bayonet. This was more than Spider could stand. He grabbed the man by the neck and tried to pull him out of the line, but all the men yelled to the sergeant, "Spider's down here trying to bust in!"

"Naw, I ain't, Sergeant!"

Johnston called down the chow line, "Spider, if you don't go to the end of the line, you ain't going to eat. Now I mean you be on the entire end of the line. And don't say nothing back at me, unless you talk so somebody know what you're saying."

Ross walked on toward the tent, as the chow line split in the middle, and the men all scrambled for new positions.

Gary stood in the door of the tent, watching the mess line. "How come they can't leave The Spider alone? I never seen a bunch of niggers act so wild."

Inside, the squad was all awake and up now. Sleeping bags had been piled on the end of the platform. Roscoe and

Snow were setting up a plank shelf on wooden horses along the wall. Skin stood over the sheet metal stove shuffling a deck of cards, while Theophilus sat unwrapping a radio from a blanket.

"Well, Ross, they tell me you going to leave us," Skin said.

"Not if Finley don't come back with the truck," Gary said.

Skin looked down at Ross' unlaced shoes. "If your feet's real bad, you might get sent clean back to England. You ought to take a nice rest."

Theophilus said, "Old Ross, he didn't used to look like that."

"Well, his nerves is tired." Skin said.

Theophilus went on, "Ross, he be smoking a cigar, hitting those rubber stampers in your service record, then the next thing he's going overseas, and fighting Old Doodoo."

Gary laughed, "Old Doodoo sure knew who to fight in this war. The Ross put him on a pension."

"I wished I had trench foot," Roscoe said in a hoarse voice. "You never would see me no more."

Snow and Roscoe finished putting up the shelf, and both lay down on it. Snow slapped his fat stomach and began to moan, "Now I lay me down on the banks of the Moselle—" They all listened. He was adding the name of a new river to his psalm. He went on, letting his voice rise and fall, "Now I lay me down on the *banks* of the Moselle, and the river runneth over—"

Roscoe sat up. "Is that where we are?"

"Must be," Theophilus said. "Snow rode in the jeep with the Lieutenant."

Snow went on emphatically, "But I will fear no evil —damn, I just remembered whose day it is in the kitchen."

Roscoe sat staring at the ground, "Is *that* where we are?"

"Big greasy hog," Gary muttered.

"That's what The Man said when we rode in together,"

Snow told them.

Theophilus began to mimic the Lieutenant, "Boys, you going to have the best billet in the whole army, a great big chat-toe, with gold beds."

"Hush up now, boy," Skin told him. "If it ain't no more room in that chateau, then we sleep in here, like we always been doing. When they were in pup tents we didn't stay around them."

Roscoe said it again, as though from deep in his lungs, "The *Mo*-zelle, my old man was always talking about the Moselle."

"Big old hog," Gary said. "Always talking about somebody's people."

"What you blowing your gums out about?" Roscoe asked Gary.

"That damn Williams," Gary said. "He know I don't play that!"

Snow began his psalm over again, "Now I lay me down on the cold mother ground—"

Roscoe laughed, "You niggers sure woke up wrong this morning."

Skin dealt himself out four poker hands on the platform and turned them over, "I was up in that little half-assed chateau last night. The sergeants took all the beds, all over the people's antique beds a-wallering and a-fighting. The rest of them is sleeping on the cement."

"—And the river runneth over," Snow said.

Ross sat down on the platform and began taking his rifle apart and cleaning it. "There he go again, folks," Theophilus told them.

Snow said, "The Ross is going to take you by your little nappy head and throw you out of this tent if you keep messing with him every day about that rifle. That's the only rifle in here you can see down. One night you going to be glad Old Ross took care of his rifle."

Theophilus said, "When it ain't for you to be doing no shooting, it might just as well be some more thundering and lightning out there—not even worth sitting up at night to look at it."

"Just the same," Skin said, "next time we load up to go somewhere, don't anybody put our poultry on Finley's truck. No telling where The Man would send him."

"The Man," Gary said. "If he's The Man, what I'm is? And Williams ain't nothing but a white-mouth. I'm going to raise a corn on his head with *my* rifle."

"Next thing," Skin told him, "they'll carry you to the penitentiary, like they did Finley's brother."

"Well, he need to be locked up," Gary told them.

"Gary, you know you don't get along with nobody out there," Roscoe told him. "If you feel like wolfing at somebody, come on in here, in the tent."

"Come on in here and do it," Skin said, "and we'll just look at you like you're crazy. Acting the way they do out there, The Man's got them eating out of his ass, and they don't even know it."

A truck turned in at the chateau gate. Theophilus looked out the door of the tent and came back. "That's not Finley. Where you all reckon Finley went after those rations?"

"Jesus knows," Roscoe said. "I hope he think to feed our chickens."

A truck driver put his head through the flaps on the tent. "You all let a man get warm?"

Skin looked around, "Yeah, come on in. That you just drove up?"

He nodded that it was, and stepped up to the stove with his mess kit and canteen cup.

"You on the Red Ball?" Theophilus asked.

"Every day," the driver told him.

"What you hauling?" Snow asked him.

"Ammunition, gas, and Germans, mostly."

"You all ain't borrowing any company drivers?" Skin asked him.

"Ain't been no days like that since August," the driver told him.

Snow told him, "We sent a truck out for rations before

we moved here, and he ain't showed up yet."

Ross asked the driver, "Where's the hospital from here?"

"They've brought nearly every one of them in England over here, now. They got one just down the road in Nancy, just set up last week, but if you can't walk, they send you to Paris."

"Lay down, Ross," Snow told him.

"What kind of outfit you all got here?" the driver asked. "I seen you got signs along the road all the way back to the Meuse River, but I couldn't make out what it was."

"Salvage. Class two and four," Snow told him.

"What do you all salvage?"

"Different things—tarps, web equipment, shoes, clothes, stoves, typewriters. We got the trailers out there full of sewing machines and shoe equipment. From here on up to the Front, you don't wear your own clothes. Everybody wears salvage."

"Before you all woke up in here this morning," Gary told them, "Johnston put the whole first platoon in the trailers."

"What the hell Johnston do that?" Snow demanded. "Those niggers are tired. I know I'm tired."

"They don't act tired," Gary said. "They're in there hunched over those sewing machines, talking about, 'We're flying over Germany!' "

Snow explained to the truck driver, "I'm out here in the cold with crazy people, and the river runneth over."

Sergeant Johnston passed by, beating on the trailers and tents, *"Let's all fall out and piss on a rock! It ain't quite day, but it's eight o'clock! Chow time!"*

The men came out of the trailers, their arms full of shirts and pants, and stumbled into the tent. They dumped them in a pile on the platform, then went on toward the kitchen.

Gary said, "Don't anybody forget his gas mask and a pro."

Theophilus dug around in his pack, "I ain't got no

rubbers. Every time it rains, those guards they come steal mine, to put on those rifles."

Gary said, "You got to show one or you don't eat. They ain't changed that."

Snow ran his hand down in his pocket, "Come on, everybody. I got a few."

Ross put his rifle together and loaded it. They were ready now, and went out.

# *III*

ROSS HAD never had questions about himself he could not answer, or had never admitted it. But today he wondered if a time might come when he would use up whatever he ran on and fall, like a buzz bomb, down into things he could not remember but dreamed about, and explode. Right now he just wanted to get the hell out of this company. How he got into it was that he was somehow unable to do his work in the records section, so he was put on shipment. It hadn't seemed important at the time, but now he would have to get out of this company, and not just to the hospital. He would have to not come back.

It couldn't just go on and on forever like this. For one thing, the company would finally get tired of wolfing at each other and start messing with the white man. There was no question in his mind that even men like the 49th Salvage might someday take on the white man, any white man. He had seen it, Post Cadre, Section II, without his having to know what happened on the army post that weekend, walking into the woods with that rifle at his back. "And it will happen that way," Ross said, "like what the French were doing to the Germans, one at a time. At the same time the colored housemaids working in white people's homes would start putting a little something in the white people's food, like my Aunt Dora used to do."

The men in his squad had become accustomed to hearing Ross just start talking all by himself, but recently it seemed to be nearly all of the time. It was not his Aunt Dora. He had been told that his great-great-aunt Dora had gone insane and had made pies for the Confederate soldiers. No one bothered an old slave woman, near blind, with a corn cob pipe in her mouth. She could climb on a mule and go where she pleased for days at a time. And Aunt Dora would ride into Confederate camps around sundown, build a fire, grease her skillet, and start making pies—sweet potato, dried apple, and dried peach, wrapped in dough. When she had finished, she would yell, "I got pies'n pies—pies'n pies!"

Aunt Dora would tie her skillet to her mule and ride on, while the soldiers died in their sleep. There was no counting how many times she had done this. Confederate or Union, white and black, all soldiers were Confederates to Aunt Dora, and all ate her pies'n pies.

And that was why Ross wanted to get out of the company, before it came to that. It was not easy for Ross to live with what he knew. "I know where being a nigger starts out wrong in the morning," he said aloud. "It's still being here when you wake up, because all night the white man couldn't figure out how to not have you here. Whatever else is wrong, or goes wrong—what somebody might say to somebody else, or do—isn't going to make it a damn bit better or worse. The colored man's trouble is he's still here, like a fool, walking around taking up space."

"Ross, you're in the chow line, now," Roscoe told him. "Why don't you shut up, before the rest of the company hears you talking like that."

For the rest of the company, the men with Ross were the last-minute replacements. Unable to operate sewing machines or repair shoes, they were assigned to sort clothing according to size, and fold and tie it in neat bundles by the thousands. The Spider was transferred into the company to replace Old Doodoo, since in civilian life Spider had been a shoe repairman. Ross and the men in the tent had to keep up with production from three trailers of sewing machines. Having done all that, they sorted what came in on trucks from other units of the battalion—two mobile combat laundry units, and the F-and-B company (fumigation and bath). Gary and Skin had already been overseas, in the Aleutians, and found this battalion hard to believe—that the military art of supply had now come to include whole companies of men who rode around behind the Front operating mobile shower baths and sewing machines.

Before the war, to hear Skin tell it, he had been out and around, even in Europe, and had been rich, none of which had much changed him, to hear him tell it, from when he started out from the swamps of south Georgia with a plain deck of cards. Skin had a song he sang, and a story he told about a slave, which had meanings for the rest of the squad which Ross could not comprehend. This was about the son of an African tribal chieftain, who came to Georgia in slavery, not by being sold into it but by his own choice, to hear Skin tell it, by taking hold of a long chain to which slaves had been tied, and walking with them into a slave ship. This was explained as the way Skin, himself, solved a variety of problems.

For Ross, Skin made no sense at all, even when he told much the same stories over and over again. In most things having to do with the company, to hear Skin tell it, they had best be on the end of the line.

The chow line moved quietly now, into the kitchen and out again. One man at a time came out carrying his canteen cup of coffee and a carton of K rations. As two men on night guard duty came out of the kitchen, the chow line greeted them with abuse.

"Don't think The Man ain't going to make you pay for it!"

"I believe he was shooting at The Man!"

"I'm going to see The Man, myself, and see he make you pay for it!"

Snow asked the men in the line what they were yelling about.

"They had Higginbotham out here on guard duty last night with Eugene Green. One of them shot a goat, and the other one shot up the Lieutenant's jeep."

Eugene Green and Higginbotham came arrogantly down the kitchen steps with their rifles and rations and sat down in the Lieutenant's jeep to eat, still with their steel helmets buckled tightly under their chins.

Snow yelled at them, "Hey! How come you shoot out that windshield?"

Roscoe told him, "Stay out of that, Snow."

Eugene Green yelled over, "You bring your big black butt out here when I'm on guard, I'll shoot you." And he pointed his rifle at Snow.

Snow waved his fist in the air, "Nigger, you don't be pointing no rifle at me! I'll come over there and drag you out of that jeep!"

Roscoe grabbed Snow around the waist, "Hold on, you're getting down wrong, messing with those guards."

Snow broke loose from Roscoe and went over and grabbed Eugene Green by his steel helmet with both hands and led him in the posture of a deep bow, out of the jeep. "Now, who you think you wolfing at?"

The men in the chow line roared with delight.

"Turn loose my head, old fat nigger—before you make me spill this coffee!"

"Who? Who?" Snow led him in a deep bow, around in a circle.

"I mean Snow!"

"Who? Who am I?"

"Mr. Snow, please, sir!"

Snow led him back into the jeep and let him sit down, "Now, tell everybody how come you to shoot up this jeep, little nigger, and don't give me no more sass."

Eugene Green straightened his helmet, *"You big gate-*

*mouth, snaggle-tooth—*" Snow grabbed the helmet "*—son of a bitch!*"

Snow led him right back out of the jeep.

"Turn me a-loose, nigger, before I throw this hot coffee on you!"

Snow grinned and nodded to the chow line for approval, and twisted the helmet until Eugene Green went down on his knees.

"You're the best, man! You're the best!"

"You going to throw that coffee on me?" Snow twisted hard, "*Huh?*"

"Ow! Naw, Snow, goddamn it!"

"Put it down on the ground. Put it down!"

Green put the coffee down.

"Now, tell the boys how come you to shoot up that jeep."

"You better *not* turn me a-loose—*Ow!* I was walking my post—"

The men in the chow line got quiet to listen.

"I was walking my post and I thought I saw something looking at me— Nigger, you better not *never* turn me a-loose— Ow! I was walking my post and I seen something looked like two eyes shining at me."

Snow told him, "That's those dials on that jeep."

The men in the chow line were now weary of laughing and yelled for Snow to let him up. Snow let go the head and walked back toward his place in the chow line, "It's getting so at night a man can't walk out to the latrine. And I never thought I'd be in a company crazy enough to dig a latrine on top of a hill."

Eugene Green ran up behind him and raised his foot to kick. Snow was expecting it and grabbed the foot, "Now, let's go on back on one foot and sit down in the jeep." Snow pulled Green along hopping on one foot and sat him back down in the jeep. Higginbotham was laughing, but Snow asked him, "What the hell you laughing at? I'll have you telling how come you shot these people's goat."

Higginbotham dropped his smile. "Snow, it ain't right

out here at night. You hear things, and those people up on the top floor, they been blinking their flashlight out the window at airplanes."

"Aw, blinking at what airplanes? Ain't no airplanes interested in the 49th Salvage." Snow let Eugene Green go get his coffee by himself; it was time for Snow to get back in line to go in the kitchen. As they started up the steps, Sergeant Johnston reviewed their prophylactics and gas masks; then they passed inside. Hughes was frying eggs and bacon for the Lieutenant and the five new white people, and Sergeant Williams stood beside a tall soup pot of coffee, with an open case of K rations on the table. As each man held out his cup, he ladled off the coffee, handed out a carton of rations, and made one of several brief remarks:

"That's all!"

"Ain't no seconds!"

"Don't tell me your troubles!"

"You want something hot to eat, suck it out your rotten teeth!" He looked up and saw Snow leading the squad, "Snow, where in hell is that goddamn Finley?"

"Don't be asking me where Finley," Snow told him. "I don't run him."

"You don't be talking to the Mess Sergeant like that," Williams said, "I'm just liable not to give you nothing to eat," and he let the ladle float in the coffee.

Roscoe said, "Yes he is, Snow, so don't say nothing back."

"I ain't going to beg him!" Snow balled up his fist at Williams, "Nigger, I'll jump over this table and set you down in that coffee!"

Williams shied back, "You'll what?" Snow grabbed his head and twisted it down over the coffee. "Watch out, Snow! That stuff's hot! I was just playing!"

Snow let go the head.

Williams grinned, "You know I was just playing, Snow." He ladled off coffees for Snow, Roscoe, Ross, Theophilus, Skin, the truck driver, and Gary; then Williams came to Spider. "What in hell you want in here, Spider?

Ain't you been through before?"

"Naw, Sergeant. That other sergeant, he made me be on the end of the line."

"Ain't nobody getting no seconds. Go head on out of here, Spider."

Hughes came over from the stove. "I believe Spider done ate, and washed out his cup. That's what I believe."

"Naw, Sergeant, I ain't eat!"

"Spider, you're a Geechee-mouth lie! Now, you get on out of here!"

Spider swung his mess kit as if to hit Williams, but Hughes got him from behind and spun him back away from the table.

Ross snarled at them, *"Let the man eat!"*

*"What you say?"* Hughes demanded.

*"I said let the man eat,"* Ross snarled again. With coffee in the other hand, he had dropped his rifle from his shoulder down across his forearm, but his rations were still in that hand. "Let the man eat," Ross said quietly.

"That's what he said," Theophilus told them, "—and that's the cleanest rifle you ever going to see."

Hughes looked at Williams, and Williams picked up his ladle. "All right, get it and get on out of here, Spider, so I can get finished."

Going back to the tent, Snow said, "One day I'm going to just mop up that kitchen with Williams."

"You act like you don't like to eat," Skin said. Wasn't none of that called for." They put their canteen cups on the ground around the sheet metal stove and sat on the platform opening paraffin-coated cartons. Skin bit into the corner of one of them and tore the lid off. "Snow, every time you step out of this tent, you start that wolfing at people, like you think you're bad enough to whip all of them."

"They wolf at me. You seen that."

"That don't make nothing," Skin told him. "And you, Ross, like you were going to put holes in somebody."

Ross and Snow ignored him and began to shake out the

contents of their cartons on the platform—packs of four cigarettes, cans of ham and egg, fig bars, square biscuits, lump sugar, coffee powder, chewing gum, can openers, and toilet paper.

While they ate, Snow began to grumble, "What I'm spose to do? You seen that."

Skin started again, "Snow, one time I was on a ship with nothing but sugar cane workers, about five hundred of us, when we ran into a storm and it just looked like the world was going to tear up. I was so seasick I couldn't hardly stand up. All I did was sit there on the deck in the middle of the boat and hold on. Well, one of the planters that was paying for the boat, he was a wee bit gone in the head. He came running down to our deck yelling all about how we was making too much fuss, and for us to shut the hell up. But actually hadn't nobody even opened his mouth except to throw up. So we just looked at him like he was crazy, which he was, until he turned around and ran back upstairs, and came back with a big fat pistol. Then he said, 'Now you niggers be quiet before I shoot everybody.' "

Snow asked him, "So what did you all do, take him?"

"Naw, didn't nobody have to take him. That's what I'm trying to tell you. We all just stood up, quiet like. Didn't say nothing, and then we just strolled on over at him, everybody together. So he commenced to backing off, till he came to the stairs. So when he went up the stairs we just went on up with him, nice and slow. Then when we all got up there he commenced to backing off to the other side of the boat, until he had his back to the rail. So we just all strolled on at him until he climbed up on the rail. And it didn't matter how crazy he was, because it wasn't nothing for him to do but jump off, or shoot, or throw the gun down. So he throwed the gun down on the deck."

"Then what you do?" Snow asked.

"Nothing. We just turned around and strolled on back away from him."

"So why didn't he ever shoot?" Roscoe asked.

"I don't know how come he didn't shoot," Skin told

them. "You have to ask him how come he didn't shoot. But I've seen more than that. It was just before I left home, the Klan marched in on our side of town. It was about ninety of them, and all of them had a pistol, a shot gun, or a bird rifle, and one of them was even a lady, because I could see her high-heel shoes. They marched on in until they came to where we were standing there in the street, like we didn't see them. Didn't a living ass move. We just stood there in the way so they couldn't go through, looking like we didn't know they were anywhere around. They marched on up and came where we could see their hoods sucking wind when they breathed, and they just stood there while the traffic light kept going red and green, red and green. Then they turned around and ran out of there like somebody had turned a-loose dogs on them. And they never came back."

Snow asked, "You all must have had something."

"Naw, we didn't have nothing."

Snow said, "Then it sure must be some ugly looking people where you come from."

"I don't know how come they run," Skin said. "You'll have to ask them how come they run."

"I know one thing," Roscoe said, "where you come from they can out-lie anybody else."

"I was standing there looking at it," Skin said.

One of the sergeants walked past, beating on the tent, *"Off your ass and on your feet! Let's all fall out in the company street! Reveille!"*

"Tell them I'm in here keeping the fire," Snow told them. "I don't want to hear that white man."

Outside the tent, the sergeant blew his whistle and from every direction a dozen other whistles began to answer him.

Snow said, "Something else I'm going to do, I'm going to take all those whistles and throw them down the latrine, like I did that bugle."

# IV

THE COMPANY was lining itself up in the mud between the chateau and the tents. The first sergeant yelled down the line, "You mens get off each other and spread out. You know how to do." The men elbowed each other until their lines were twice as long. "Tea-*hut!*" The men banged their heels together up and down the line, and threw their chests out. "Reee-*port!*"

Two hundred men—the night shift, the day shift, and the shipping room crew—were all present or accounted for.

The Man came out of the chateau in a pair of coveralls and leaned against the handrail of the kitchen stairway. There had been one other lieutenant and a captain, but they had both managed to cut out of the company as soon as they got to England, leaving the question of why this one white man had stayed. He always started reveille by giving them a long look in silence; then he said, "You boys fall out and gather around these steps here, so you can hear what I'm telling you." They fell out of rank and took off their helmets to sit on them before The Man. "Now, as you all see, I kept my part of the bargain. This is the best billet in the army. You can forget about pup tents for a while. Now, I know most of you lost your pup tents in the river, but I'm going to have Sergeant Neal write all that up as lost-in-combat."

The men murmured approval.

"That's right, this is considered a combat outfit, and we're in the combat zone. Now, I want to see you keep your part of the bargain and keep that production schedule where it ought to be. Now, when you show me you're ready for it, I'm going to see if I can't scrounge around and get up some passes and furloughs for some of you, but for right now, this company is *re*-stricted to the area, and I don't want to be a-having to keep a-telling you what that means. Unless you're going to the latrine, stay in the yard. Now, I'm going to see if I can't get some Good Conduct medals for everybody that haven't given me any trouble, and I'm going to see if I can't get hold of some Bronze Star decorations, just like any other company. But I ain't a-going to go out of my way to get nothing if you start a-screwing up, and going down in that town around those filthy women, catching clap and coming in here to me having to go to the hospital, and drinking that cognac. You know you haven't been used to anything like that back home, and it won't mean anything but trouble with me. Now if every man keeps his eye on the next man, nothing is going to happen. Now, I've given the First Sergeant a list of promotions to post on the bulletin board. That's just a start. Show me what you can do." He paused to let the men think about all that. No one seemed deeply interested except Ross. These morning talks made him ill. A vile taste flowed into his mouth. He hated the Lieutenant, feeling he had to because no one else did, and it frightened him that he found it harder and harder to do.

"Now, the order just came down from higher up, you're not supposed to dig any more foxholes. Sergeant, will you remind the boys of that?"

*"Ain't no more foxholes, men!"*

"Now, I expect a load of salvage in here sometime this morning or afternoon so the shoe squads can go to work. The rest of you can work on with what we brought from the last area until it comes. That's all."

The Lieutenant turned and went back into the chateau and the First Sergeant stood up. He looked around through the men sitting before him. "Where's Spider? Private Spider Jones!"

"I ain't no private!"

"You better look on the bulletin board and see what you is. Sergeant Williams say he want you to git him a garbage pit."

"Sergeant, what I do? I ain't do nothing!"

"*I*-said-Sergeant-*Williams*-said git him a garbage pit by sundown."

"Yah-sur."

"And don't *sir* me. Now, the company clerk has some mail to read off."

The men cheered and stood up, and the company clerk came out on the kitchen steps, "All right, at ease!" He held up the first one, "I got one from Lily-Mae!"

*"Here!"*

The men laughed and passed the letter back.

"I got one from Bernice!"

"Aw, nigger, call the mail right! That's my mama! I don't play nothing like that!"

The men roared and the company clerk stood with his hands on his hips while the letter was passed back.

Ross, Skin, Roscoe, and Gary started back to the tent, leaving Theophilus to listen for mail. Inside, Snow was writing pants-size numbers around the wall of the tent with a piece of chalk: *32, 34, 36, 38*—. Waiting for the end of the mail call, they stood around the stove, passing a bottle of cognac from hand to hand. Finally a roar went up outside, and the first platoon marched past the tent toward the trailers.

"Well, I guess that's all she wrote," Snow said.

Theophilus came into the tent, empty handed, "The Man's out there and coming right this way."

They hid the bottle and took up positions around the platform to fold clothes. Snow went to peep out the door, "Maybe he'll go the hell on by— Atten-ch-*hut!*"

The Lieutenant poked his head through the flaps and came in. "I wanted to tell you boys in here, you been doing good. Now, I don't have any more p.f.c. stripes, but Jones just lost his corporal stripes. I don't know which one of you runs things in here. I think it's about time you knew, and I knew. I'll leave it to you to work it out, and then one of you come tell me. I'll have the company clerk add his name on the list." He turned to go out of the tent, "That's all. You can go on back to work now."

The men looked at each other and sat down on the platform. Gary said, "Why you reckon the Lieutenant went and did that? That wasn't called for."

Roscoe said, "What are we supposed to do, flip for it?"

No one answered. They just sat.

Skin jumped up and grabbed off his helmet and dashed it on the ground. He began to dance wildly around swinging his fists in the air, "Naw! We ain't sposed to flip for it! We sposed to get out here and lock ass and fight!" He wiped his nose down the whole length of his sleeve and raised his fists to a boxer's guard, "Snow, git up! I'm sposed to break your jaw."

Snow lay back on the platform, "I don't want to be no corporal. We ain't never had nobody in here. Go tell the Lieutenant we don't want no corporal stripes."

Theophilus said, "That ain't no way to act when somebody gives you something. Ain't no use throwing it away."

Roscoe raised up off his arm and looked at Theophilus, "Little nigger, you go to hell."

Skin smiled, "Naw, now wait a minute. One of us could have that little piece of money."

Roscoe sat up, "I'm going to throw *both* of you out of this tent."

Skin pulled out his cards and began to shuffle them, "Hold on, now. Hold on. That boy's right. We don't have to *have* no corporal."

Gary said, "Yeah, but what somebody going to do with any money? All mine goes home, except four dollars a month. I don't hardly find no place even to throw that away."

Skin studied the idea, "Yeah, that's right." He turned the cards off the deck one at a time. "We all got it in lotments. But ain't but one of us got children."

They all looked at Snow.

"What you all looking at me? Don't look at me. I ain't going to be no corporal."

Theophilus said, "Yes, you is."

Snow waved his hands furiously in the air, "All I get out of work is a tired feeling!"

Skin smiled, "Naw, it ain't neither."

"—And when I get tired, I likes to set down! I don't

want to be chasing nobody, telling them what to do!"

Skin smiled at him, "Snow, you remember what you told me when they had us working on the docks in Liverpool?" Snow was silent. "Man, you were kicking that two-wheel truck around like it was a limousine! Talking about, 'These bales of clothes sure do handle good,' and bragging about how you could flip one right into place without straining yourself, cause it was an art to it."

"Well, that's work!" Snow told him. "That's different from this. This ain't no work, just standing in one spot all day, folding shirts as fast as you can. This don't do nothing but make me tired. Yeah, I liked being on the docks. That's my sport."

"See what I was telling you?"

"Well, that's work! But this ain't no work. Ain't nothing in here for a man to grab up and throw on his shoulder and tote off, like it was a sack of coffee." He threw his chest out, "I could load coffee all day." He got up to show them, "You go and you grab a sack by the ears, see, down low, and then you kick your knee in it and it rides right up on your shoulder. Then you tote it off." He tracked by them, bending over with his hand on his hip. "That's my meat! And cement. That's a good one, and any kind of beans, and little coal you can scoop, and potatoes when they're sacked good. I don't like to mess with no mail. It'll fool you, cause it's just liable to be a piece of iron, or two hundred magazines. But nice size boxes and crates that don't get all broke up, that's good. And watermelons, that's good. Everybody lines up and if you turn your body right, they shoot down the line and nobody can feel any weight."

He stood in the mud, grunting and turning his body the right way, with his hands under watermelons. "See that? Then it's gone to the next man, and you turn around and meet one, then it's gone. Now, that's work! If it's anything I hate, it's working up beside somebody that can't work. It's people like that. They don't mean nothing by it. If you ask them, they'll tell you they can't dance, neither. They don't feel no rhythm."

Snow went into a soft shoe routine, grunting a tune for accompaniment. Skin said, "Snow, go head on and tell The Man you going to be the corporal."

Snow stopped in his tracks. Gary said, "Go head on, Snow. Ain't nobody going to ask you to tell them what to do."

Roscoe told him, "You get proud, and I'll bust you back down, myself."

Snow stood looking at Roscoe, then pulled off his combat jacket and spread the sleeve smooth on the platform. In the place for the chevrons he chalked: $.

Snow went out of the tent putting on the jacket, and the men went to work folding and stacking shirts and pants under the size numbers along the tent wall. As the stacks built up, someone took away ten and tied them in a tight bundle with a tag giving specifications. They worked swiftly and deftly, cutting the process to the least number of movements. As the pile began to disappear, men from the trailers came in with armfuls more.

They worked smoothly, feeling the flow of clothes from the Front down through the battalion—for fumigation, laundry, and repairs, and then across their platform to the shelves, and bundles.

Skin would begin to sing, *"Oh, we don't even know his right name—"*

The rest would join in, *"No, we don't even know his right name—"*

Skin would stomp his foot and clap his hands off the beat, *"Nicodemus took hold of that chain, and we don't even know his right name—"*

Theophilus would send his voice up high and slide back down, *"Well, we—"*

All, *"—don't even know his right name!"*

Roscoe would send his voice down and ride up, *"No, we—"*

All, *"—don't even know his right name, Nic-a-DE-mus took hol-a-dat CHAIN! And we DON'T even know's right name—"* and they worked on, singing as though compelled by the bounce of the rhythm, snapping a finger when a hand was free, making faces as they played over the vowels, snaking a hip as they turned to the pile of clothes.

When they stopped to eat again, the rose bushes were cut down in the other storage tents, the bundles were moved there, and through the afternoon trucks rolled in from the battalion.

Late in the day, Gary came in and announced, "Yon come Finley." They listened as the truck shifted gears, and came in through the gate, then backed up to the kitchen.

The men worked on quietly, waiting for Finley to come in the tent.

## V

FINLEY POKED his big head through the door of the tent and pushed the chicken box through in front of him. He stood up grinning and finished eating a banana. "You all been waiting on me?"

The men didn't answer.

Gary went over and lifted the chickens out of the box, one by one, and stood them on the platform. "They act like they can't stand up."

Finley looked at the chickens as though for the first time. "I'm sorry I couldn't get in here no quicker. They had me out there—"

Gary snapped him up, "What the hell is sorry!"

Finley looked around at the rest, "What you all looking at me? I couldn't get here no quicker."

Gary took up one of the chickens on his lap and began to stroke its head, "These chickens is sick, Finley!"

"I *said* I was sorry."

Snow asked him, "Where the hell you been all this time, Finley?"

Finley tossed his banana skin into the chicken box, "They had me out on the Red Ball."

Snow told him, "Nigger, you're a lie, and the truth ain't in you! You ain't been out on no Red Ball!"

"How the hell you know?"

"One of those drivers was in here this morning and *said* you wasn't on no Red Ball!"

Gary joined in, "That's how come niggers don't never have anything. Somebody all the time messing up."

Skin asked him, "Finley, what happens to you when you get out on that road? You ought to stay around the tent here, where somebody can talk to you."

Gary said, "I don't want him in here. It's about time we put him on out of here before he do something else." He looked at Finley. "Finley, go head on out of here! We don't want you round here no more!"

Finley stiffened, "Who going put me out?"

Gary jumped up, "Nigger, I believe you wants to fight!"

Finley took off his helmet, "Go head on. Put me out. I believe you can do it."

Snow jumped up, "Nigger, you know Gary's too little for you. Let me see you whip my ass!" Snow and Gary grabbed Finley high and low, and tried to drag him out of the tent.

Finley planted himself with an arm around both of them, "If you wants to get bad, it ain't nobody badder than me! It ain't no two of you badder than me!"

"It ain't no two people drunker than you," Theophilus told him. "Man, you smell like the running nausea."

Snow yelled to Roscoe, "Roscoe! Come help us throw him out!"

Roscoe watched them but did not move. "Aw, man, don't throw him out. You'll have half the company in here."

Finley got Gary down in the dirt, but Snow hung on to Finley's head. Gary yelled up to Skin, "Skin, tell Finley he can't be in here no more, before I have to get up from here and kill him!"

Skin stood up trembling. "Now you all stop all that! You ever see how pigs do it? Come a time when it's too cold to be wallering in the mud, they all up together and put one down where they can all sit on him, and from then on that's the nigger in the bunch. When you go out to feed them, they always got that same one bound down. Once *they* ever find out which one it is, ain't a thing you can do to put fat on him. That's the way straight out and out pigs do it!" Skin stood with his knees trembling, not sure he had said it right. The men stopped, not sure what to do with themselves. Finley picked up his helmet and went on out of the tent. Skin took out his cards to shuffle them, but his hands were trembling and the cards fell to the ground. No one picked them up. The men went and sat down around the platform, not looking at each other. Then Gary wiped the dirt off his face and said, "Well—go and get him."

No one objected. Skin wheeled around and poked his head out of the tent, "Hey, Finley! Wrench out your mouth and go tell the Lieutenant they done moved those ration dumps, and you just had to go round till you found it."

The company clerk came in, trying to figure out what they were all doing. "Ross, the Sick Book is ready, any time you want Finley to pick you up and go. If you all have a load of salvage ready, move it on out when he go."

The company clerk went away and Ross began talking with himself about the fight he had just seen, and about Akela, and Post Cadre, Section II. Then he turned to them with a question, "All that fighting and the white man wasn't even here?"

Roscoe said, "You know, we might not see old Ross no more till we come out of the army."

Gary said, "Ross, you have a nice time in the hospital."

Snow said, "Ross, if I ever have a shingle over my head, you know you got half a shingle."

Skin said, "Ross, you get in a white company where you can make it."

Snow asked, "You reckon they'll let Ross do that?"

The truck backed up outside, and the men lined up to toss the bundles. Skin said, "Snow, now this is where you shine."

Snow hopped up into the back of the truck, "I told you I ain't sposed to be folding those shirts. O.K., let them come."

The bundles moved steadily, one behind the other, until the floor of the truck was packed, almost to the tail-gate. Snow jumped down and Finley came around to shut the back of the truck. He called to Ross, "Get your stuff, Ross, and let's go. The Lieutenant say you hold your rifle on The Spider till we get to the Stockade."

Roscoe asked, "The Spider? What he do?"

Finley said, "What the Lieutenant told me, Spider dug a hole and Williams come messing with him, so Spider took and split his head open with a shovel."

Theophilus asked, "How come you ain't taking Williams?"

"I'm just supposed to take Ross and The Spider," Finley told them. "Ain't nobody can lift Williams. He's sitting in that hole. The Lieutenant, he say they going to leave him down there and just shovel him up."

"What's going to happen to this company?" Snow asked.

"Jesus knows," Roscoe said.

"I hope you all eat," Finley told them. "Hughes say he ain't liable to fix nothing."

Ross got his rifle and dug around in his pack until he found his wallet, some old letters, a pencil, then changed into a clean pair of trousers and shirt from the piles along the wall. The Spider was sitting quietly in the front of the truck. Finley and Ross climbed in with him. Ross wished he could tell The Spider he was sorry he had to hold a rifle on him until they got to the Stockade, but he was not all that sure he hadn't come to hate Spider just the same as everybody else outside his tent. That was the real reason he wanted to get out of the company.

As the truck pulled away through the mud, the shipping room crew followed behind as far as the gate. Finley shifted gears and left them standing there as the truck pulled up the long hill.

Roscoe asked, "How come didn't nobody else get his feet messed up? We were all there when that river cut loose."

Skin said, "I sure hope they think to look at Ross some place besides his feet."

Snow said, "You reckon they'll let Ross in a white company?"

Theophilus said, "They talking about they going to desegregate the whole army, but Ross don't want to be round no white people."

"Nor you niggers, neither," Snow told him.

Roscoe said, "That Spider, he sure messed himself up."

"Jesus knows," Snow said.

# *Desegregation*

# *VI*

DESEGREGATION IS a negative act, a stepping backward from the wreckage. You are permitted to take nothing of your own with you. Where desegregation would not have been permitted, it still happened, constantly, anywhere some other requirement needed every attention, as now when Ross found himself swallowed into the belly of a world unknown to him, and he fixed his attention upon its walls. Down a blackboard coursed brown rivulets of water vapor condensed in tiny drops that grew until their weight was enough to move one into another downward into deltas on the loops chalked with soft crayon. Then they streamed on, moving bits of the letters from their paths into canals that dropped in puddles on the floor. Ross decided that in a few days the words would all be gone. They were not important words, a class assignment—the date was five years old. The room was heated as never in all its winters. The French had held classes. The Germans had brought casualties, but the Americans had brought stoves as well, for they had oil to burn.

Ross looked at the men around him, lying in litters on the bare floor—clinging to charred steel helmets rimmed with the scum from shaving in hard water. And one in bathrobe and pajamas limping toward him, carrying an armful of dirty clothes. Trembling from the effort, he flopped down on the next litter beside Ross. "When you have to stop in the middle of a shower bath and come set down—you're tired!"

One of the nurses followed him out of the bath. "I thought I told you to leave your clothes in the salvage!"

He winked at Ross and tried to stuff them inside his bathrobe. "They sure got you where you can't sneak out in the town."

The nurse sorted out his clothes over her arm. "You won't need clothes where you're going." A set of dog tags fell out of a pocket. "And put those around your neck, soldier."

"Hey, wait a minute. You can't take that sweater. That ain't issue. That was hand-knitted by a movie actress."

The men on the litters around him stopped shaving and laughed. "Don't get her mad at you, fellow!"

"She'll put you to mopping the floor!"

He sat watching his clothes being snatched piece by piece out of his lap; then the nurse picked up the bottom of his bathrobe and looked under. "What's that you're sitting on?"

"That? That's one of them new type of field jackets. It ain't many of them been issued."

The patients cackled with laughter as the nurse snatched it from under him.

"I can empty my pockets, can't I?"

She handed it back. "Go ahead, I've got no time to argue. All right, one more of the rest of you guys, go bathe. And *don't* wash your feet. They'll give you bathrobes and pajamas down the hall."

One man got up from his litter and limped off to the showers while the rest watched the combat jacket pockets being emptied: one bent pewter demi-tasse spoon and a roll of toilet paper from down the hall. He turned to Ross, "When you had your bath, they didn't issue you no house shoes, did they?"

The nurse told him, "No walking around in here, not even to the john."

"Aw, all right, lady." He went on with the pockets: one sterling silver salt shaker, one can of meat-and-beans, half a loaf of French bread, one mustard pot, an English-French dictionary. . . . She picked up the jacket and shook it: eight onions, one cheese, six packs of cigarettes, and matches.

She walked away.

"Oh God, hey lady, wait a minute," he called her back. In a side pocket: one army issue road map of France, printed on silk.

The nurse went off in the direction of the salvage pile, and he turned to Ross and extended his hand, "Ed Webb is my name. Knoxville, Tennessee. 5th Division. Are you Infantry?"

"Ross," was all he said. They shook hands. Ross was not accustomed to shaking hands with white people. He could think of nothing further to say.

Ed Webb looked around among the rest of the patients. "Hey, any you guys got any foot powders? Any talcum powders?"

Everybody laughed.

"Any alcohol? I been rubbing them with cognac, but that stuff don't do no good."

Ross didn't see anything funny about Ed Webb, so he took his old letters and his pencil out of his bathrobe pocket and pretended to read. He had read them many times before, and a page of one letter was lost:

*. . . here to go overseas, and you'd think that now, with the invasion on, if people were ever going to act right, they'd do it now. I'm sorry for the Major that he hasn't got any better sense, but some people are never going to learn anything, or act right. Anyway, this German came into the dispensary on sick call. He had never been in before. But I remembered this one. He was the one I said told me he had*

*expected to see our people wearing tiger skins, carrying knives in our mouth. I was sitting here at the typewriter and you could see how it hurt him to have to stand at attention in front of me. (Smiles) I made out his hospital tag: NAME, RANK, SERIAL NUMBER. There aren't many blanks you can fill in for a prisoner of war. ORGANIZATION: Stockade. Then I gave it to the Major to write in DIAGNOSIS and TREATMENT, but like I said, some people would rather die than act right. When he brought it back to me, there was one more blank filled in. RACE: White. Honestly, it's just some of these people that will simply have to get killed.*

*Slap me a Jap,*
*Rick*

Ross folded it, and put his letters back in the pocket of his robe. He looked at the paper tag on the clean white string around his neck. Only *Name, Organization,* and *Serial Number* had been filled in, and *Diagnosis: Trench foot. Both mild.*

He took the pencil out of his pocket and beside *Race:* he wrote faintly *white.*

It was as simple as that, he told himself, but it wouldn't be. Now he would have to make up a whole new story about himself, as if he was some kind of a secret agent. One of his uncles must have done that. He must have planned it out for several years. Then one day they found a note from him. He was going away and had a job waiting for him, but the family was supposed to act as though he had died. He never did come back. And it wasn't just his uncle. A lot of his relatives had done that.

A black soldier with his arm in a plaster cast came toward Ross, "Hey, buddy—"

Ross looked up at him.

"—you got a dry match?"

While Ross fumbled in the pockets of his robe, Ed Webb struck one and held it over, "Ed Webb is my name. Knoxville, Tennessee. 5th Division."

"Joe Johnson's mine." He sat down on the floor between the litters, and he and Ed Webb went on talking.

Ed Webb smelled himself. "My clothes sure did stink after I came out of that shower bath."

Joe Johnson laughed.

Ed Webb asked him, "Boy, how'd you bust that arm?"

Ross lay on his litter pulling on his tag. He might say he was from Chicago, but he didn't know anything about Chicago. Maybe he'd better erase it. The rest was all in ink, anyway. He asked Ed Webb, "Have you got a fountain pen?"

"A what?"

"Nothing. Forget it."

Ross erased *white,* shoved the pencil deep in his pocket, and lay blinking in a cold sweat. The room began to swim. Joe Johnson was talking, "—And I put my truck into Brest when it still wasn't nothing up there but tanks, not even any infantry." Ed Webb tried to cut in, but Joe Johnson went right on, "I've walked away from seven wrecks. One time I jumped out of a load of gasoline just before a plane blew it up. And then four of us trucks piled up on each other in a turn just the other side of Rheims. We don't have no governors on those trucks. You can get eighty miles an hour. And sometimes you have to—" He punched with his fist, "—bust out your windshield so you can see. I was the third truck in that line. It was coils of barb wire bouncing up and down all over the road."

Another black soldier with a small piece of adhesive tape above his left eye came over and joined them. Joe Johnson asked him, "What they tell you?"

"Ain't nothing wrong with me. Come on let's go out and find something."

Joe Johnson introduced him, "This is my driving buddy, Homer Brooks."

"My name is Ed Webb. Knoxville, Tennessee. 5th Division."

The patient in the next litter lifted himself with difficulty, "Tom Shanahan, 4th Armored."

Ed Webb said, "You still ain't said how you come to bust your arm, boy. You do that knocking out windshields?"

Homer and Joe exchanged looks. Joe said, "It was this fool here, was driving."

Homer Brooks grinned, "Who? I wasn't driving." He asked Ross, "Can I sit on your bed?"

"Sure, go ahead," Ross told him and moved over so Homer Brooks could sit on the edge of his litter.

Joe said, "There wasn't another nothing anywhere on the road."

"You know I wasn't driving. You was."

Joe looked down his nose at him. "I'll be damn if I'll take you out on a pass with me no more."

Homer rubbed Joe's head. "Old buddy, you know I wasn't driving, you was."

Shanahan lifted himself on his elbow, "Hey, who the hell was driving?"

Homer and Joe pointed at each other, "He was."

The men on the litters around them laughed. "How many of you all was driving?"

"Sounds like it wasn't nobody driving!"

Ross didn't see anything funny about the two drivers. They were putting on a show in front of white people.

Homer told them, "Well, my old buddy here, he don't know too much about jeeps."

Joe lifted the arm in the plaster cast as though to strike Homer with it, "I believe you'd even go back and tell that to the Captain. That's the last time you'll ever drive me anywhere."

"Aw, now buddy," Homer said, "I'll see you get another pass." The two of them began to scuffle as Joe tried to poke Homer in the stomach, and Homer rolled back giggling, against Ross' feet. He turned to Ross, "Oh, excuse me, soldier!"

Ed Webb asked Shanahan, "How in hell does a man get trench foot in a tank?"

Shanahan asked him, "You ever get locked up in a meat ice box?" and began telling Ed all about tanks.

Homer straightened out the blanket and asked Ross, "You in a tank outfit, soldier?"

Ross hesitated, "49th Salvage."

"I think I know somebody in that outfit. A big-head boy, used to drive on the Red Ball." He turned to Joe, "Joe, who was that big head boy, used to be an extra driver, was in the 49th Salvage? His brother cut a whore in Montereau."

"Finley?"

"That's right, old big head Finley."

"I know him," Ross admitted. "He's in my squad."

Joe frowned. "You ain't in no 49th Salvage."

Ross flushed with anger and told him, "What do you say we don't bunch up."

Joe stared at Ross and said, "All right, you baby-shit-colored nigger, each to his own." Then he and Homer got up and walked away.

A ward boy came to the door and yelled, "All walking patients can go to the movie! Be back here at eleven o'clock!" Homer and Joe walked out of the room with the ward boy.

Ed Webb told Ross, "Aw, you shouldn't have told the niggers to leave. You know the army is fixing to put one in every other foxhole?"

Ross wanted to ask him what he had said, but he had heard it and didn't need to hear it again. "They were sitting so I couldn't stretch my legs out," Ross told him. Shanahan was in the middle of telling Ed Webb about tank warfare in the North African desert, and drew his attention. . . .

*You ain't in no 49th Salvage*. . . . There had been a lynching, right on the army post, only a few months before he was drafted. They found him hanging from a tree over the swimming pool, behind the service club, bleeding into the pool. . . . The voice said, "Where you think *you* going?"

"I'm going to the service club to get a beer," Ross told the other patients, his eyes fixed on a light bulb that hung from the ceiling. His mouth hung open, and short, painful groans came from deep within.

A nurse bent down over him with a glass of water and a blue pill, "Here, take this," she said. "It'll make you feel better and get it off your mind."

Ed Webb told Ross, "Look all around, boy, see? You're in the hospital, now. You're all right, now."

Ross said to her, "Nurse, I want to go back to my company. I'm not sick."

She laughed at him, "Well, we're not going to worry about that, are we?"

As the nurse went away, Ed Webb put his arm around Ross' shoulder, "I've heard fellows talk brave before they've been up there, but this is the first time I've heard somebody talk brave coming back. Hell, it's so many of them up there now, they don't need you. They're walking all on top of each other. Your name was Ross, wasn't it? Well, you might be interested in this—I was just telling these fellows sitting here with their faces hanging out, when I first came in the army, I didn't take no notice of what I was giving up. I actually didn't realize what I was doing. It was just something new; like new clothes somebody might give you —until the third week, and then I went to a moving picture show in the post theater. Well, I was sitting there just a-laughing and having me a good time, and when it came time for it to be about over, I was saying to myself, 'Well, next thing I'll do, I'll go cross the street to the drug store and have me an ice cream.' But when the lights came on, I looked around and it wasn't nobody in there but soldiers! I wasn't nowhere near that drug store! I was in the army!"

Shanahan said, "Aw, that's no scary story."

Ed Webb said, "I don't know why not. I thought I was sitting in the moving picture house in Knoxville, Tennessee, and when the lights came on, I was in the army!"

The men kidded him. "You got to do better than that, Ed."

"Yeah, Ed, you're talking to soldiers."

Ed Webb raised his hand, "Don't discuss it. Me and my buddy, Ross, here—we've had a belly full." He turned to Ross, "Call ourself celebrating Halloween, trying to tell scary stories, but don't nobody know one. You know any?"

Ross shook his head, no.

"Well, how about this one? We were in a rest area in

some little frog town back there, I forget the name—had been a French cavalry barracks before the Germans got it—"

Shanahan said, "This one better be good."

"—And there was a piano on the first floor. Well, quite naturally I set down and commenced to play, and then the whole outfit, they come over and we started singing. Well, it went on like that for about an hour or two, and then they all commenced to banging on the keys so I couldn't even hear what was me, a couple of them on each side, so I said to hell with it and went to bed. Well, the next morning I was going to steal a march on them, so I came down real early before breakfast and sat down and was playing away when I took notice of how flat some of the keys sounded, so I took the front off of it. And what do you think I saw?"

"Six Heinies in there had you zeroed in," Shanahan said.

They all laughed.

"There was enough T.N.T. in there to blow the whole building to kingdom come, and wired up to the lowest note on the piano."

The men were silent.

"And you know, I'm afraid that just about ruined my musical career. I don't believe I could touch a piano no more."

Shanahan said, "Well, boys, it looks like we've been saved."

The men laughed. Ed said, "Just for that, I hope we get sent where it ain't nothing for us to do but sit up and smell each other's feet."

Shanahan said, "That a man can get used to."

"Aw—! You haven't ever heard me play!"

"Don't you two bust up our Halloween party!" the men yelled.

"What'll we do next?" Ed Webb asked them. "What else do people do for Halloween?"

Shanahan draped a towel over his face, "Boooooo!"

Ed Webb said, "Boy, you look better that way than you

did before. What you supposed to be, the Hunchback of Notre Dame?"

"Boooooo!"

"You look more like the Ku Klux Klan," Ed told him.

The Halloween party went on, and Ross took the other letter out of his bathrobe pocket and began to read it.

A girl in his class in college had written him that she was starting a small magazine. She was paying a local white printer to handle the job, there in her home town, but the printer hadn't liked some of the material, especially one editorial, yet remained oddly silent about it. A few days before the magazine was to appear, Ross got a three-day pass to visit her, and the girl's grandfather put him up on their farm.

More had been known about the magazine than they realized, and on the third day, as Ross drove her to the printing shop in her station wagon, the whole town stood out on the streets and watched them arrive. Then they found out why. The whole printing job had been carefully smeared with ink. Not a page of the magazine was legible, and she had paid in advance.

She was furious. It no longer mattered to her how she spoke to the printer. Ross had to take her by the arm and drag her out to the station wagon. For this she was angry with Ross too, and argued with him all the way back to the farm. Two hours later, when he had to catch a bus and go back to the army, she refused to take him to town. He walked back, and found it completely deserted. Down the main street and down all of the side streets he saw no one. Even the drug store that served as the bus station was closed, but he had a round-trip ticket and waited for the bus. It was late that same night that he was walked into the woods behind the service club.

She never answered his letters, and he finally stopped writing. Then after a whole year—

*Dear Paul,*

*As you see, I have left home. Your mother writes that you are overseas. I am sorry that I have not written, but I didn't know how to say what I have to say. I am sorry about that argument we had about the magazine. I have tried to forget the whole thing, and I hate to write this way because you are overseas defending this country, but I want you to know what happened that night you left. I should have told you long ago. Paul, when we came out of that printer's office, that was the signal for the Klan. Even Grandpa knew, but he was afraid to tell us for fear of what we would do. He knew you had to be on that bus. I am ashamed of myself for not driving you back to town, but it was the only reason you got out of there. Believe me, I honestly didn't know. Grandpa walked out and met them in the peach orchard, by the second barn. He was just an eighty-year-old colored man who never made anybody any trouble, and they beat. . . .*

Ross looked up. A nurse was standing over him. "What are you?" she asked.

He refused to say.

"Well, don't get mad at me. I didn't do it to you. Let me see your tag. You're trench foot? You get two of these." She handed him two large white pills and went on to Ed Webb.

A doctor started down the outside row of litters, examining the patients and writing on their tags. Ed Webb threw the map he had been reading aside, "Look half-dead, everybody. Here comes the principal to mark our report cards."

Shanahan said, "You talk like you've been through here before."

"Nothing to it. If he's halfway lucky, a soldier can spend half his time in the hospitals. I was hit already three times. Now if you get *Ambulatory,* like the two nigger boys, that means you can walk, and they just keep you around. But if you get *Communication Zone,* then you get the works, three meals a day in bed, a wheelchair, and a pretty little nurse to keep care of you."

The doctor uncovered Shanahan's feet. One was mild, but the other was swollen and split like a boiled sausage, and the toes had shriveled and blackened, ready to fall off.

Shanahan was embarrassed to have them all looking at it. "Doc, what's the scientific cause of that?"

"Bad circulation due to lack of proper care. I know it's a hardship, but you men should never allow yourselves to fall asleep with your shoes on."

Ed Webb broke in, "—And I be damned if that ain't just the way I was brought up at home."

The doctor skipped the lecture and went on marking tags.

Shanahan read his tag and asked Ed Webb, "What the hell is *Z.I.?*"

"Zone of the Interior. That's America, boy."

When the doctor turned toward Ross, he closed his eyes as though he were sleeping. He felt a tug at his tag; then the doctor went away, and another tug and Ed Webb said, "Well, I don't know about the rest of you, but me and Ross here, we drew the Old Soldiers Home."

Ross wanted to look at his tag. He waited as long as he could bear it and then opened his eyes. *Treatment: Com Z, Height: 5'9", Weight: 170, Race: W,* all in pencil.

# *VII*

ROSS SAT reading his tag again and again. The doctor had done it himself. At any rate it was done, and he leaned back on the litter with the tag lying on his chest, wondering what to do next. He took the two letters out of the pocket of his robe and struck a match to them. The damp paper curled slowly into the flame, and he dropped them on the floor. Getting up from his litter, he tied his bathrobe and picked up his towel and soap. He thought he would like to go stand under the hot shower again. When he came back, he would start to live his life all over again.

He walked between the litters and passed a patient kneeling, smoothing out his blanket—slowly, deliberately, going over it again and again, and here and there he stopped to slap the blanket and speak to it. He looked up at Ross. "You'll never get clean in there," he said. "It's the soap, they make it from people, fat people."

Ross kept away from him and went in the shower room. He turned on the hot water, took off his robe and pajamas, and stood under the water until he was warm and began to relax. "The French are different," he mused. He had enjoyed French in high school, and his college French professor had lived in France. He wore a beret. Ross imagined this small black man with his little beret, walking the streets of Paris. "Learn French! French is the way around all of this!" the professor used to say. "The French are so civilized!" Then tears would come into the professor's eyes, and he would thrust on the little beret, his scarf and overcoat, and thrust himself out a classroom window and down the fire escape to walk alone on the campus. His students all worked extremely hard because it meant so much to him. Ross thought, "Perhaps when the war is over, I won't go home." He began to sing in the shower, the song Skin had taught him, "Nicodemus took hold of that chain . . . and we don't even know his right name. . . ."

He wanted to sing, but he couldn't think of a *Race: W* type of song. He remembered, "*Allons, enfants de la Patrie,*" and he sang that. He didn't really have to stay in France. Like his uncle, from now on he could go anywhere, except home. He went on singing, "*—Liberté, Liberté chérie, Combats avec tes défenseurs. . . .*" His face became serious.

They had baptized him at an Annual Church Convention. During most of the Convention, he had been allowed to go outdoors and play, but he'd had to sit in the big auditorium and watch the final session. Someone was to be elected the National President for the coming year, and two ministers had been nominated for the job. Each was to address the Convention before the voting. The first one to speak had very light skin, and when he rose to the platform there was only sparse applause, and when he had finished, even less. The other preacher was very dark, and as he rose to the platform he received a great ovation. His speech was long and loud, and he rushed up and down the platform waving his hands while the people in the auditorium shouted, "Amen!" And when he took his seat the audience rose to its feet and cheered. Ross did, too. He'd liked the speech although he had understood none of it. And he wanted to vote so he could vote for the second speaker. But as the auditorium became quiet, he saw the light-skinned preacher go to the rostrum and Ross was afraid that he was going to try to say something bad about the second speaker. After he raised his hands for silence, all he said was, "Ladies and gentlemen, before you vote, I want to introduce my wife. . . ." And a little black lady stood up from the audience and took a bow. Everyone applauded and the auditorium buzzed with whispers.

"—And my opponent's wife. Will she stand up, please?"

After a long hesitation, a light-skinned woman with red hair stood up, but no one applauded. The auditorium became very still, and the preacher went back to his seat and sat down. He won the election.

Ross turned off the shower and began to dry himself, then slumped on a bench in his towel. "There is nothing to go home for," he said.

There had been a girl. It all started when he was in the fifth grade, when he announced to his parents that when he grew up he was going to marry Tillie. They were all seated at dinner when he said it. The maid was clearing away the dishes. She stopped, and rolled her eyes at him, "That Tillie's as black as I am. I didn't raise you to marry no black gal."

His parents told her it was no way to talk to the boy, but before that dinner conversation was over, it was obvious that this feeling, if not quite the maid's expression of it, was what he faced from his parents.

To find a black face on either side of that family, one had to look back six generations to people like his Aunt Dora's mother, who was half white. Before that, nobody knew. And as Ross grew older, he was no longer surprised when he heard the same sentiment from others, like his Aunt Dorene, his father's sister. She pleaded with him when he was in college, not to do what his twin blonde cousins had both done. They had rebelled against her, she told him, and gone out and married "the blackest thing they could find, and were miserable!" But as early as when he was in the fifth grade, it was clear to him that someone must also have said something to Tillie, for there sprang up between them a fake show of antagonism in front of other children, even hostility—always with an attempt not to be too convincing. There would be a look, or a smile, meant only for each other, which said, "When we grow up. . . ."

She became beautiful at seventeen. She was slim and graceful, and her hair was a soft black fluff that he wanted desperately to touch, but they were never alone. And then, one day before their high school graduation, she came to school with her hair as straight as his. The girls crowded around her, but Ross sulked away by himself, thinking that it looked like nothing so much as a drowned rat. His anger about this disappeared when he heard that they were both going away to the same college. Yet even there the pretense continued.

He couldn't see the reason why, nor was he now sure that it was pretense, or that it had ever been, for they had never put their feelings into words. He would try to be friendly but she would be hostile, except of course that there was always somebody standing nearby. He dated other girls, smug, light-skinned girls, girls that his parents said he shouldn't mind having to marry in a hurry, if he had to. After all, his parents knew all their parents, all the women from the same sorority, except that by now they would let in a very dark girl if she was an exceptional student. The fraternity he was expected to join, but never did—it had been his father's fraternity—also operated on the same basis if a very dark boy was smart, or had money. But Ross became lonely. It was spring, and everyone on campus was coupled off, walking arm in arm, or lounging on the library steps.

Ross decided that he would walk the whole campus from end to end if need be until something happened, some smile, some look, from Tillie. On and on he walked, examining every face, until he came to the hill and the Science Hall. And there she was.

She was coming toward him from the top of the hill. He could tell that she had seen him. And as they walked toward each other, he realized that they were alone, alone with this whole section of the campus to themselves in the middle of the day. He knew that she had also noticed this, for she began to prance as she walked. It was the way they had said such things to each other when they were children. As he walked on, his loneliness turned to a dizzy warmth within him. They both walked faster, and she seemed to hold her arms out to him, and smile. There was something wrapped in paper in her hand. Ross could not be sure—maybe she meant they would run right into each other's arms. He rushed on, his arms outstretched to her, but as they met, some wet, foul-smelling thing hit him in the face. And he walked on and on and on, and did not ever look back. . . .

"Why did she? It's no mystery," he said. "She hated me. Hit me in the face with a pig embryo soaked in formaldehyde, and no one was even looking."

Ross noticed that he was mumbling to himself, and dressed in his pajamas and bathrobe to go back to his litter, now baptized into a new man. He opened the door, but when he saw the others lying in their litters, he slammed the door and leaned against it while he put his tag around his neck.

Someone began pushing against the door, trying to get in. Ross stepped aside and it was the one who had been smoothing his blanket. He stood blinking at Ross, with a faint smile; then he asked, "Give me a drink of water."

Ross elbowed past and left him there. He wondered for a moment how he would get his drink of water out of the shower, but he wouldn't go back to see. He went to his litter.

Ed Webb had a crowd around him. He was saying, "—And seeing as how one of our good brethren is leaving us, namely Shanahan here, and since they're going to carry us out and put us on the train sometime tonight, for which all them pill-pushers have left the room, maybe we can get started on this!" He pulled out a long bottle and the men cheered. "Hold on! Hold on! If we get to making too much fuss, we'll wind up giving this stuff to a ward boy."

Shanahan took the bottle and worked out the cork, "Well, boys, all I know is I'm going home!"

As the bottle went around, Ed Webb said, "I didn't tell you what those two nigger drivers told me. Like I was saying to Ross here, we got to act right now, because the army is fixing to put one in every other foxhole." The bottle came to Ross. "Well, it seems they were on a pass and got boozed up, and one said to the other one, 'You better pull dis jeep back over on de right hand side of de road!' And the other one looked at him and said, 'Ain't you driving?' " The men roared, Ross took a drink, a good big one, and handed the bottle on. He saw the crazy one who had gone in the shower, coming out with his pajamas and robe all wet, still smiling, and mopping at himself with swift, delicate hands. Ross was sorry now that he hadn't helped him, and in shame turned over on his litter, away from the Halloween party. Between the drink, the bath, and the blue pill, he sank into sleep. . . .

Two black litter bearers lifted Ross gently from a rack on a boxcar wall and prepared to carry him off the train. As he stirred in his sleep, one of them said, "Hey, man you ain't supposed to be asleep. You're in The Gay!"

"In the what? Go to hell, Skin, let me sleep. . . ."

The other litter bearer frowned at him, "Man, this is Paris!"

*"Oh!"* Ross leaped up and almost off the litter.

The litter bearers laughed and mimicked his *Oh!* and Ross was wide-eyed as they carried his litter out into the crisp morning air, across railroad tracks to an ambulance where he was lifted in and the litter strapped to the wall. Two other patients in litters were placed on the floor beneath him, the door slammed shut, and the driver pulled away into city streets.

Ross lifted himself forward on the litter almost to the driver's shoulders so he could see. At the first corner the sign said *Rue d'Alsace,* and then *Boulevard de Magenta.*

Ross had drawn in the main avenues and boulevards on a college exam but could not recall Boulevard de Magenta. He wondered exactly where he was and how much more he would be able to see before they got to the hospital. He searched for some monument or building that he could recognize from all of his professor's post cards. Down a street to the right, he got a glimpse of another railroad station, *La Gare du Nord.* At the next corner the driver turned to the right and through the gates of *L'Hôpital Lariboisière,* it said. They had arrived. It seemed like a palace at first, with its high iron gate and the armed guards. As they drove in, he saw there were two buildings side by side, with an enclosed garden between. His litter was rushed down an arched hallway and into an elevator that inched slowly up and up to *Salle Bazin.* He was carried through swinging doors and to the edge of a vast white bed, and was told to climb in.

Dawn flooded through polished windows as he sat watching the rush of French and American nurses placing the in-coming patients. American nurses wore simple brown dresses, but the French wore white linen scarves that fitted tight across the forehead and hung down behind, and linen aprons taken up in tight folds all across the back, and Dutch wooden shoes they would step out of and go sliding along the white tile floor in black wool stockings. One of them came to Ross and began to help him out of his bathrobe. *"Comment vous appellez-vous—eh?"* she demanded.

He responded immediately, "Paul Ross."

She spoke slowly, as to a foreigner, "Aaah! You speak French! I can come back and talk to you." She pulled open the sheets at the foot of the bed, rolled a pillow into a ball and placed his feet on it. Then she tightened the sheets so only his feet and ankles were exposed. "Now you must not catch a cold. Remain just so. And where did you learn French?"

"In school."

"Aaah! A student! And what do you think of France?"

Ross hesitated. "I have seen nothing but the woods." It was a poor sentence, but she got the idea. She was about to leave and he tried to think of something more to continue the conversation. "And what do you think of the Americans?"

She laughed hysterically and went away, leaving Ross to look around the ward. He saw Ed Webb and was glad not to be at the other end of the ward with him. Then he noticed one black patient, and he remembered his hospital tag.

He would have to decide now where he was from and what school he had gone to. He took out his wallet. There was nothing of importance in his wallet, a few invasion francs, his civilian driver's license. He pulled it out and read it: *Race: N.* He tore it up. His YMCA membership card. It didn't say *Negro,* but someone might know the *Hartley Street Branch.* He tore it up. His public library card: *Wilson Street Branch.* He tore it up. A celluloid calendar. He turned it over and read the back: *Your kinky hair worries are over! Have straight hair always! No hot irons. No lye. New safe formula.* He tore it up. And down under everything else there was a newspaper clipping:

*I have been reading your column and I enjoy it but that is not what I am writing to you about. I am writing to ask you to help me and others who are in the position I am in. My mother was Negro and my father is white. And I am very light. In fact, no one would suspect me of being Negro, but I don't deny it. Yet if I don't, I can't get a job, and I find it hard to get along with both races. When I am with whites, they resent me because of my dead mother, and Negroes don't accept me. It always ends with "If I had hair like that—" I really don't know what to do. I am twenty years old, and engaged to a very nice white boy and I'm afraid to tell him. It really wouldn't mean anything to him one way or the other, and it wouldn't mean anything where we both work now, because they have just started hiring Negroes. But what can I do? Wear a sign? I am working in an office where they think I am white and living with white relatives because of the job, but how can I tell him? I wish someone would help me.*

*New York, New York.*

*(signed) Troubled*

Ross had kept the clipping almost a year. He had thought of writing to her through the newspaper, but realized he couldn't solve anything, either. At first, he thought she should marry someone very dark, the way his twin cousins had done, so people would know. But with his cousins, people still thought they were white, only more than before. Everywhere they went somebody said something. It was pretty obvious that *Troubled* just wanted to be white. None of it made any sense. He tore it up.

Except for a few invasion francs, there was nothing else in the wallet. He stuffed all the bits of paper into the pocket of his robe. In the evening after the room was dark, he got up to throw them into the toilet, but his feet would not bear his weight. He was unable to walk.

In the morning, as the French nurse was washing his face and hands, he gave the bits of paper to her. "I tried to walk last night, and I couldn't stand up," he told her.

"You tried to walk? Oh, don't tell the American nurses. They will be furious!" She went on to shave the next patient. "You Americans. Such asceticism! You can endure any hardship but a cure!"

Ross wondered what she knew, if anything, about the condition of his feet, but soon he was merely looking about the room. He could not talk with the patient on his right. This was the one who made his bed. Ross watched him for hours on end as he smoothed out one sheet and then another, and the blankets, one by one, and when the bed was finally made, it was time for lights-out.

The patient to his left was unable to look in his direction. He was in a plaster cast that began around his ears, forcing his chin up, and came down over all of his body to his elbows and knees, holding his arms and legs out and away from him. His bed was of no use to him except as a place to rest his feet. The cast hung by chains from hooks in the ceiling, and was open in the seat so the nurses could help him use a bedpan. Taped to the window behind his bed, like panels of a stained-glass window, were X-rays reproducing this posture. In the center of one, across the spine, was the jagged image of a piece of metal.

Ross was brought food. Sometimes he ate it, or played with it. No one spoke to him except the French nurse. Even the doctors did not talk. They merely came by once each morning and pushed against his toes, and then walked on.

All day bursts of laughter came from the other end of the ward. He was unable to hear what they were saying. No one had looked at his hospital tag, and it didn't seem to have made any difference to be a *W*. The only jokes that were passed along from bed to bed far enough for him to hear were: *Air raid* spelled backward is *diarrhea,* and *one in every other foxhole.*

One day a small group of cabaret musicians and entertainers burst through the swinging doors of the ward, singing as they came and playing saxophones, clarinets, and violins. One man carried a bass fiddle, another pushed a small piano. They went on playing, toward a vacant space at the back of the ward, doing several numbers without interruption. A girl in a tight evening gown strolled along the aisles, singing to each as she passed.

When they asked for requests, the men at the other end of the room yelled for Ed Webb to play, and the piano was pushed beside his bed. Before he began, he lifted open the front of the piano and looked inside. Everybody laughed. Then he played a slow waltz. The musicians caught it and played along with him. After two choruses they began to push the piano away, slowly, toward the door, still playing the waltz, and they all bowed as they went out, the girl last.

She blew a kiss with both hands.

Eventually as the days passed, a crate was brought into the ward and opened on the floor. Men on crutches and in wheelchairs carried back to their beds magazines, books, decks of cards, dominoes, flutes and harmonicas, and writing paper. There were also Christmas cards to send.

Ross waited for the moments when he could talk with the nurse. He smoked, slept, and read. Sometimes one of the younger French nurses would puff up her hair and smooth out her apron, then come down his aisle with a mop, or bring him a bedpan, having decided that here was one *beau garçon* who had done something about the war. He would watch them arrive, each with a look as though there was something he ought to say first, before she would reply to him. He had no idea what that was, because a polite *bonjour,* or *merci,* got no response, and actually seemed to anger them. And the same one would never come near him again.

It went without saying that French was a language he knew; yet this was not different from how it had been in New York with several languages he did not know at all. Ross was not sure he could survive in New York. Alone, in uniform, on a twelve-hour pass, just the day before going aboard a ship to come overseas, he had been followed along 42nd Street by a man speaking to him in Spanish. Ross had stopped several times and explained that he did not understand Spanish, until the man became angry and said to him in English, "That's the way it is with us—we get a little money and we don't speak Spanish any more." Following that, Ross had wanted to have lunch in an Italian restaurant. He had never been in one before. But the waiter became livid and walked back into the kitchen without taking his order because Ross did not order in Italian. Several people had then peered out at him through the kitchen door, and a dishwasher came forward, speaking to him in Hindustani, so Ross had lunch at a Walgreen drugstore.

Often Ross thought he might ask for a wheelchair and

go talk with the one black patient. Ross would watch him go in a wheelchair to play chess with an English pilot. Ross could see he was English because of the Royal Air Force uniform hung over the chair beside his bed. He was the only one who had any clothes. Ross guessed that the English didn't have any salvage.

Thanksgiving Day had come and passed; then one day in December he saw his French nurse again. She stormed past, muttering to herself. Ross called after her and she turned with her hand over her mouth. *"Vous avez compris?"*

He smiled and nodded that he had, "Something about American nurses breaking your feet?"

"But you won't tell them."

He assured her no, and she began to talk. "Those stupid girls of yours! They say I am not qualified to read a thermometer! Took it from my hand! So I simply dropped it and broke it! And I will break six more things before today is over! Six! You watch me! I went through a war in this hospital before they were born! But German nurses and doctors were more polite! They had at least the grace to say, 'If you approve, madame,' and 'Will you please, madame,' and 'Thank you, madame!' "

He laughed at her French with a German accent, and she laughed with him. She pretended to be arranging his bed in case someone was looking, "You don't live in a place, you Americans, you visit. Then you leave. And one day I think you will leave America."

"Why do you say that?"

"Oh, I have read, and I have seen. I used to go a lot to the cinema. I could tell you about America—about Jean Dillengier, and hot jazz, and penicillin, and what vagabonds you are! You are like the weed you sing of, the weed that tumbles. It is the way of your social and economic life, entirely! If I came to America, I would have only to invent a way to make something portable, and I would be a millionairess!"

Ross explained, "We have a big country, long distances from place to place, but France is small."

"Yes, I know, I know, but America was built by people who—you will excuse me, but I feel this—who in time of their trouble in Europe, ran away. Why run away across thousands of miles of ocean and take a jungle from a poor savage? Is that a brave boy?"

"But here there was persecution—"

"And none in your America? Look what you do with the blacks! Persecution, yes," her face became stern. "All the more reason to stay in Europe. When the Germans came, my husband never thought to go to Canada. We are not Canadian. We are French!"

She left him to go on about her work. But Ross thought about their conversation for several hours. Only four months before, a German would have occupied this same bed. And she was here through all of that. She has a lot of guts, that woman, probably went around nights like Aunt Dora, blowing up bridges.

His Aunt Dora's mother was as far back as he knew his father's side of the family—there were no photographs of her. He tried to imagine her, a half-white teenage girl, sold to a whole wagon train of men so poor they all had to chip in together to buy her. She was taken into Kentucky, and for years never saw the sight of another woman, white, black, or Indian.

Of all her children, Aunt Dora and her sister, Selene (Ross' great-great-grandmother), were the only ones who had been able to stay together. Grandma Selene was sold alone to a slave trader Ross had found in library books. Among his many enterprises was the purchase of good-looking quadroon women for resale to the Quadroon Ball Room, a gentlemen's club in New Orleans. The slaver and Selene started down the river for New Orleans, but they never got there. He married her. She had a child by him, then starved him to death locked in his own cellar. Grandma Selene went out after that and bought her sister Dora, but somehow or other never bothered to set her free.

Ross lay in his hospital bed trying to think of a man locked in his own cellar until he starved to death, and of

Grandma Selene carrying him up to his bed when he was dead. He was old and rich, and she was young and good-looking.

Late in the day, the nurse returned to him, offering an apple. "I should never have talked to you that way. Of all the people, you American boys. You would stand and face anything. Not like some of us. You will forgive me?"

He accepted the apple from her. "But you've fought the Germans."

"But I am a nurse. There was little I could do."

"Like blowing up a bridge?"

"Such a violent boy, I would never dream of blowing up a bridge."

"But you did do something."

She leaned over to whisper, "Perhaps we were not always as efficient as the Germans, a bit neglectful—things were lost, or left unclean, or disappeared, or allowed to spoil, or dropped and broken—oh, I broke so many things of the Germans. Light bulbs were very dear, and eye glasses, and false teeth, and burettes, and a microscope, and vaccines—not easy for an old nurse to learn such things. And one had to be always careful of the Germans. They are very observant. Now you eat your apple. I have told you too much as it is. But please forgive what I said. You American boys, you can regard yourselves without shame."

As she went away, he wished that he had told her that he was black, and he was ashamed.

"I'm a dead man back in those woods behind the service club," he told himself, "or I would be if that guard hadn't dropped the rifle." Was it because he lost his nerve? He looked up at his hospital tag clipped to the chart above his head. "It wouldn't work. I might say the wrong things. Suppose people started talking about what they did when they were kids, or about their families. Would I talk about Aunt Dora and Grandma Selene? Tell them Tillie hit me in the face with a pig embryo? Tell them why?" He had made himself tired. "There's got to be somebody I'd want to see again." He searched his memory. "Skin," he said. He never understood much that Skin was saying, but he would want to see him again—Skin never hated anybody. Ross tried to relax and forget it all; then he took the tag down from the chart, got out his pencil, and erased the *W*. In its place he wrote *N*.

# VIII

WHEN THE old nurse came to visit him again, she found him looking out the window behind his bed, but there was nothing to see between the X-rays taped to the glass—the cold, gray, December sky, the curls of lazy smoke from crooked and bonnetted chimneys on roof tops, and tracks in the yard of the Gare du Nord.

"What are you looking for, Paul?" she asked.

"I might never see Paris. I was looking for the Eiffel Tower."

"You have been deceived, this is the north of Paris. The Eiffel Tower is in the west of Paris, by the Seine. You look away from it."

She saw a loneliness that nothing seemed to fill. Kicking off her wooden shoes, she went sliding along the warm tile floor to the back of the ward and returned with a wheelchair.

"For me?" he asked.

"Yes, get up. Get up and get into the chair. I will wrap you in a blanket to be warm." He moved his feet gently into the chair and climbed in. When he was ready, she pushed him slowly down the aisle to the other end of the ward and back again, babbling French in his ear so fast he could hardly understand—little orations like those made to the tourists before the war, about Notre-Dame, the Conciergerie, the Jardin du Luxembourg, and Faculties of the Sorbonne.

Ross enjoyed the game, but she did not stop when they had returned to his bed. They went through the swinging doors and continued out past the elevator to the edge of a long flight of steps; then she turned him around and stopped before the hall window.

Across the hospital courtyard and high on a hill beyond was the dome of Sacré-Coeur. They looked in silence. "Often I go there," she said. "You would like Sacré-Coeur. Many Americans go there."

"At home we don't have that."

"Oh, at home you have many things we don't. You have industries and science. Since the Liberation we have heard of so, so many things for the first time. There is the penicillin, and the blood plasma, and—"

Ross stopped her. "I should have told you this. About the plasma. I take pride in that."

"Oh, you have worked on this discovery? You, Paul?"

"No." He hesitated. "It is the work of a Negro."

"Ah, you are a friend of his. You were his student."

"No, I never met him." He was determined, "What I mean to say is—I am a Negro."

"How so?"

Ross began to perspire. "That is to say, I am really a Negro."

"Ah! Forgive. You have contributed a donation for this research?"

"No. I am a Negro."

She looked at him bewildered; then she said, "And how do you feel about the penicillin?"

"But that's different! A Negro didn't do that!"

"Oh, no, no, no, no, Paul. The penicillin is just as important as the plasma. I think sometimes they put the penicillin in the plasma." Ross would now have been willing to let it pass, but she asked him, "And do all the Negroes feel this way about the plasma?"

"Well, yes."

"And the penicillin?"

Ross banged on the arm of his wheelchair, "No, you don't understand. Listen to me. Now, you are French."

"I am French."

"And you are proud of—of Pasteur."

"I am proud of Monsieur Pasteur."

"And he is French."

"He is French, without doubt." She thought a long moment, then laughed but saw Paul was annoyed. "My Paul, Monsieur Pasteur does not belong to France only. He belongs to humanity. In these times we are grateful to anyone who makes a good thing."

"Not everyone is, when it's a Negro."

"Tell me Paul, what has it been for you in America?"

"Once the Ku Klux Klan wanted to kill me, but I got a bus and went back to the army."

"But you, Paul, why would they want you? You are not black."

"The law says I am. And I would want to be—I have ancestors who—"

"Oh, I can't follow you. If you are asked what you are, you should say, 'I am myself, of course.' That is definitive, *non?* And of ancestors, ideas, inclinations, positions, sometimes more this, more that, but always you remain you, *non?*"

The elevator door slammed open and two litter bearers crowded past Ross and the nurse, carrying a patient who was badly spattered with mud, all over his hospital pajamas and robe, and weeping breathlessly. They banged on through the swinging doors into the ward, and an American nurse came running up the stairway behind him. "All right, let's have this hallway! You've got no business out here!" And without slowing her pace, she swept Ross and his wheelchair away from the French nurse, and on through the swinging doors. As they went toward his bed, she said to him, "You shouldn't talk to the French nurses. You keep them from doing their work." Ross made no reply. "When you sympathize with them, you can't get them to do anything. They do little enough as it is."

Ross turned in his chair to face her, "What were they doing here before we came?"

"They weren't nurses. They don't have their diploma."

She stopped at Ross' bed and he climbed out of the chair. He said, "They must know how to do something besides mop the floor."

The nurse's eyebrows raised and then dropped and came together, "Very well, if you can't leave them alone, I'll see if I can't have you moved. I don't speak French; otherwise I could handle them. They're filthy, deceitful, and lazy—always losing and breaking things!"

Ross said, "When the Germans were here—"

"Exactly," she agreed with him. "When the Germans were here, I'll bet they knew how to handle them," and she pushed the empty wheelchair down the aisle to the back of the ward.

The new patient was still crying. They had put him in a bed four down from Ross. A steady stream of new patients, mud-spattered and dazed, were being brought in. The nurses rushed back and forth placing them in available beds, until the ward was filled. But the litter bearers continued to appear with more and stood about putting them down and picking them up, until the French and American nurses got into a furious argument, his friend being the loudest—all about the Great War and the Battle of the Marne. The French nurses won, and reluctantly the American nurses instructed the litter bearers to leave the rest of the new patients in their litters on the floor between the beds.

The patients in beds began questioning the ones on the floor. The litter bearers had started at the back of the ward, so there was not anyone on the floor yet beside Ross. He kept hearing the word, *Liège*. The one who had come in crying was quiet now and sat up in bed being given a cigarette.

"What happened?" they were asking him.

"Hospital too full up there?"

He answered loud enough for all to hear, "There ain't any more hospital up there! It's sick guys all out in the fields! Buzz bombs coming over like rain!"

Others were now crowding around his bed. "How come they pulled you out of Liège?"

"We were getting those crazy-looking things—three or four a day."

"Naw, I tell you! Naw, I tell you! It's coming down like rain!" He went off the edge of the bed and began to crawl, between their legs, out of his pajama pants, dragging his blanket with him. "Oh, Lordy God, it's coming down! It's coming down!"

An American nurse ran over and pinned him to the floor with her knee, rubbed a wad of cotton on his behind, and gave him an injection. He went limp and rolled over. As two ward boys lifted him back in his bed, she waved the hypodermic needle at the patients standing around, "You guys clear out and leave him alone! They had enough trouble with him on the train!"

"What's happening in Liège?" one asked her.

She refused to say; then her voice went out of control, "The word we got is, the Germans are coming all through our front lines—" She bit her lip and stalked out of the ward.

After supper, a ward boy came in and read from a sheet of paper. He read as loud as he could and still not mispronounce the words; then he read it again:

*On a forty-five mile front, an overwhelming enemy force pressed forward five miles, between Echternach and Monschau. Also in the vicinity of Trier, Allied armies were forced to retreat.*

That evening, doctors trooped back and forth along the aisles. Nurses stood about full of impatience, or suddenly chased back and forth after the doctors trying to make themselves heard. No one asked any more questions. The patients sat counting packs of cigarettes and deciding what book or magazine to keep or leave behind. Then litter bearers appeared, droves of them. They stood around with their litters, waiting for orders, and finally they began at the front of the ward, taking some, leaving others.

Ross was jolted down the stairs, through doors, into the crisp night air, and into an ambulance. Over his driver's shoulders all he could see was the ambulances ahead and on each side of him. When they reached the railroad station, the street was filled with men and women in uniform, and civilian girls. There was music from a loudspeaker. As his litter was dragged out of the ambulance, a cheer went up from the crowd. Instead of carrying him indoors, the litter bearers put him down on the sidewalk and went away. The crowd moved in around him, blocking his view except straight up into their faces, smiling down and saying nice things in French and English. Then the crowd shifted as the litter bearers placed another litter beside him. And while the crowd ran cheering in another direction, he was taken for a long, jogging ride through the dark empty railroad station and into a boxcar, where his litter was strapped to the wall.

It was damp and cold in the boxcar, and there was no light, even from the door. He heard railroad tapping noises, then the hollow footsteps of litter bearers as they brought someone else in. With nothing else to do, he curled up in his blankets and went to sleep. . . .

The boxcar jolted and he realized that he was moving. The boxcar jolted again, banging against the rest of the train, and a few of the others woke up. Lights were on in the car. A voice heavy with sleep demanded, "Where the hell are we, now?"

A ward boy was washing porcelain cups in a sink next to a chemical toilet. "We're getting into Carentan. You'll be getting off here. Bunch of hospitals."

"Carentan?" another man asked. "I remember this town. We took it way back last June. We must be almost all the way back to the water."

The ward boy said, "We're about four miles from the English Channel. You can smell it outside."

Other men on each side of the car began to wake up and stare down from their litters. Ross recognized only the black patient and Ed Webb, both still asleep, perhaps one or two others—the rest he had never seen before.

Someone said, "It sure is restful to wake up in the morning and look down and see a floor on the floor."

"It ain't mud, brother. Hey, Sergeant, what time you got?"

"About five-twenty," the ward boy replied.

"What's it doing outside?"

He pulled open the heavy door. "Snowed all night, but it's stopped now."

He left the boxcar door partly open and Ross could see German prisoners standing with litters on the ice-glazed cobbles of the depot platform, scrubbing their gloved hands together and pulling at their thin tunics.

Someone said, "I reckon we're the ones that had the worst."

"Yeah, mud is hard as a rock when it's froze."

"Hey, pill jockey, how about some breakfast?"

The talking woke up Ed Webb. He raised himself on his elbow, then propped himself against the wall and sullenly viewed the car. "Hey, you," he called the ward boy, "quit rattling those cups and fix us some breakfast."

The ward boy turned to them wearily, "No, you'll have your breakfast when you've all been moved into the hospital."

"The hell you say!" Ed told him.

"We're hungry now!" the others joined in. "It's four o'clock in the morning—you know back here they ain't going to fix nothing."

"It's exactly five-twenty-three," the ward boy announced.

"These bastards in the Rear act like it's out of their own pocket," Ed Webb announced.

The one in the litter above Ross smiled down, "How about some of those sugar cookies in the carton?"

"I'm not supposed to give those out this trip."

"What the hell, you can get some more, but we sure'n hell can't."

Ed Webb waved back his blankets and balanced himself up on sore feet. "I ain't going to beg him."

"The Captain said none of you were supposed to stand up!"

Ed Webb made his way to the cookie carton and sat on the floor to eat. The other patients clamored to be thrown cookies. Ed tossed them into their litters by the handful, until the boxcar was powdered with crumbs and broken and rolling cookies.

With his mouth crammed full, one of the men called down to Ed, "Soldier, you shouldn't ought to have took the Sergeant's cookies."

The patients exploded crumbs and laughter.

The ward boy ignored them and opened the door wider to set out his thermos boxes. "All right, boys, just don't tear up my train."

Ross lay back down with a cookie that had fallen on his blanket. Growing up, he had heard it a thousand times, "White people are so nice to *each other*." Black people were always saying that. But he could tell now that they weren't, not even to each other.

A pretty young Red Cross worker in neat wool slacks put her head in the open door, "Have I been in here, yet?"

"Why no, honey child," replied one of the patients, mimicking her Southern speech. "You all just come right on in!"

"Hey, whatcha got, lady?"

"Bring some doughnuts, blondie!"

The ward boy helped her in with her big pot of coffee and basket of doughnuts, and got down his white porcelain cups. Ed Webb picked himself up off the floor, "Whereabouts are you from, ma'am?"

She looked back at him as she passed out two doughnuts to each man, "Memphis, Tennessee."

"Well, I'll be dog! I'm from Knoxville! Ed Webb is my name, Knoxville, Tennessee, 5th Division."

She explained that she had been there a couple of times and how dreadful cold it was in the Smokies. And did he ever know the Reverend and Mrs. MacLaren on Martin Mill Pike?

He didn't ever know them.

"It must be dreadful awful up there where you were." She asked the ward boy, "Do these all have trench foot too?"

"Yeah, the whole train. All got trench foot. That's all's wrong with them. Nothing wrong with their appetite, or their mouth."

"I wish I could go up there and see the Front."

"Well, we sure wish you could, lady."

"Any you fellows from up around Liège? My boy friend is stationed there."

"That's where—that's where it's supposed to be in the Rear, ma'am."

"What kind of outfit is he in, ma'am?"

"He's a lieutenant in the Air Corps."

"Oh! A glory boy!"

"What have officers got that we ain't got?"

"Time for women."

"I bet you wouldn't pay him no nevermind if he was just a plain soldier like us."

She was running out of small talk. "Well, I guess I'll have to leave you fellows. I got to give the others some coffee and doughnuts before they unload the train."

"Aw, don't go yet."

"Hang around. They ain't going to unload."

She picked up the empty coffee pot. "No, I've got to go. The rest of the girls need me," and with that she was out the door. She poked her head in, "Bye-bye, boys!"

"Bye, blondie!"

"Don't get married on us!"

"I won't."

She was gone.

The ward boy took out a broom and started sweeping at one end of the car. There were half doughnuts, his white porcelain cups, magazines and empty cigarette packs, matches, butts, and sugar cookies.

"Doughnuts," somebody sighed.

"Yeah, sugar-coated doughnuts."

"I'd rather had it in the coffee," another said.

"Yeah, that's the way they do. When they sugar the doughnuts, they don't put none in the coffee, and when they put it in the coffee, they don't put it on the doughnuts."

"That's the Red Cross for you."

"What do you expect for nothing?"

"What do you mean for nothing? Ain't I out here getting my feet rotted off for those people?"

"Most of the time it's in the coffee. Those were the first I've ate with sugar on them."

Ed Webb said, "Sure was a nice looking little Memphis gal."

"Nice gal from anywhere."

"It's usually somebody's old dried-up granny."

The black patient asked the ward boy, "Would you be a good fellow and give me a glass of water?"

Ed Webb looked at him, "Oh, almighty God."

The men laughed.

The ward boy got a cup of water and handed it to him. Ed Webb muttered, "What the hell you got to be around here, some visiting foreign royalty? Nobody asked me if I wanted anything."

No one replied.

"That's what's wrong with this country," Ed told them.

The black patient asked him, "What country are you talking about?"

Ed Webb fumed, "You know what country I'm talking about! I'm talking about the States! What outfit are you in?"

"Paratroops."

"Yeah, I know. I seen your badge pinned on your bathrobe."

"Then why ask?"

"You could have picked that up somewhere. I don't know. Where'd you train at?"

"Benning."

"You from Georgia?"

"No."

"No, I guess you ain't, or you'd a never growed up. You from up north?"

"No."

"Out west?"

"No."

"Well, you just ain't from the States."

"You skipped the east," he told Ed.

"Up north is east—now I know you ain't from the States."

With the others, Ross listened, knowing that Ed Webb was spoiling for an argument. He began to pull nervously at the tag around his neck; then he remembered what he had written on it. He stared at the *N*, and felt in the pockets of his bathrobe for his pencil, but couldn't find it.

Ed Webb said, "Well, what army are you in?"

"The American Army."

"You just now told me you wasn't from the States!" Ed Webb winked at the men around him, "So where the hell are you from?"

"Haifa."

"Where's that at?"

"Palestine."

"You don't look like a Jew. You look more like a half-Mexican nigger to me."

"I am not a Jew," he said crisply.

Ross dug furously into his pockets and through his blankets but the pencil was not there.

Ed Webb brightened, "A-rab?"

The black patient ignored him.

"Egyp-tie?"

Ross was terrified. He wanted to destroy the tag, but they were all expected to have one.

Two Germans entered the boxcar and went to Ed Webb's litter, balanced his weight between them, and headed out the door. Ed Webb sat up and yelled back, "Well, what the fuck are you?"

"I'm Syrian," he said. "You remember that."

Two more Germans came to the door of the boxcar. They took the man who was above Ed Webb, and as they went out, two more came in and took Ross.

# IX

THE COLD gray edge of morning hung loose along the outskirts of the village. The column of frost-glazed ambulances puffed out thick clouds of steaming exhaust. The corporal in charge of meeting the train stood in his jeep, shouting, "Hey! You two! Don't set that man down in the snow! Hey! Fill up this ambulance first! Over here!" He pointed with his flashlight, "Goddamn it, here!"

The Germans replied in English, "Yes, sir."

"Vera goot, sir."

An ambulance door opened in front of Ross and there on the wall, with another patient, was Ed Webb. The prisoners lifted Ross in and placed his litter on the floor beneath them.

Ed Webb leaned down to Ross, "He didn't have me fooled. I knew he wasn't no nigger. A nigger like that wouldn't have never growed up."

The door opened, another patient was placed on the floor beside Ross, and the driver pulled away into the road.

"Aw, I knew he wasn't no nigger, all the time."

Slowly and silently Ross' hands went all over his litter, feeling for the pencil. The one beside Ed Webb asked, "What's the matter with that one? He don't talk to nobody."

Ed Webb whispered, "Him? Special orders. Seen him burn them right on the floor, when we first came in the hospital. No telling what he's been through."

"Oh?" He thought about it. "What kind of orders is that?"

"You know, special orders. Speaks French as good as they can. Wasn't in the hospital half an hour before he was begging everybody to let him go back up there. Now there, my boy, is a soldier. I was right there and heard it. I didn't think I'd ever run across something like that, except in the movies, but that's one of them. Came in wearing a uniform looked like it just came out of the laundry. They must had to loan him one so he could come in the hospital."

"You know, Ed, if those Krauts capture a man in civilian clothes, they'd mess him up so his own mother wouldn't know him."

Ross gripped the sides of his litter until the cloth began to tear. For a long while there was silence in the ambulance, through the snow-covered streets, past the town hall, and out into the open country. Then Ed Webb said, "You know, a foreigner would rather be anything in the world than a nigger. It don't matter how black he is. Once at home there was this big buck African, came to speak at the nigger college and got lost wandering around downtown. Well, it wasn't long before he was doing wrong, and when folks came after him, he started talking about how he wasn't no nigger, said he was a British subject, and he wasn't going to sit in the back of no streetcar with the niggers. He was so black he was purple."

"I don't believe I ever saw a nigger that black."

Ed Webb said, "Did I tell the one about the nigger that hung a lamp over his front door?"

"No, tell it, Ed."

"Seems he was in the habit of coming home drunk, so he hung this lamp over his front door so he'd know which house was his. Well, he come home and he said, 'Well, dis is my house, cause dat's my lamp.' He went on in with the lamp and he said, 'Yeah, dis is my house, cause dat's my wife in de bed with me. But if dat's me in de bed, who in de hell is dis standing here holding de lamp?' "

"Ed, you must know a million of them jokes. You ain't

give out since you came to Paris. I know them, but I just can't remember a joke until I hear it. Oh, my Aachen back! Ed, look out there. You reckon this is the right place?"

The column of ambulances had turned off the highway toward a group of tents draped with the flag of the Red Cross. German prisoners stood waiting in the snow. Ed Webb was furious. "I ain't a-going to stay in no tent city. This is winter time! That ain't no place to recuperate!"

The Germans hauled them out of the ambulance and began to carry them away. Ed Webb slapped the edges of his litter, "*Git*-dap there, dern you! It's cold out here! *Git*-dap there!"

Between the tents there ran carefully laid duckboard walks branching out in every direction. The prisoners took Ross to a tent with a wooden door built into the flaps. After saying something to each other in German, they took him in. It was dark inside except for the glow from a pot-bellied stove. All the beds were empty. Ross crawled off his litter into icy sheets and thick new blankets that smelled of moth balls. The door opened at the other end of the tent and a nurse came through, putting on lights. "Oh, hello. I didn't know they had started in here, yet. Been here long?"

Ross shook his head, no.

The nurse puffed up his pillow, "What are you all tense about?" She rubbed his neck and shoulders and he began to relax.

"Are you our nurse?"

"Looks like you've got a private nurse, unless I can scare up some more patients. Would you like that?" Her soft warm hands made him shudder. She smiled at that and pushed his hair out of his face, then walked out of the tent.

A few minutes later, the door opened again and a procession of men on litters were brought in and put into beds—men from the train. There were four of them in all, and as soon as the Germans left, they began to yell, "Hey, ward boy!"

"Hey, ward boy!"

"Pill pusher!"

*"Heeeey!"*

The door opened and a gray-haired corporal came in, smoking a cigar, "All right, hold your water!"

"Hey, bring me a duck!"

"Me, too!"

"Me, three!"

He went on through the tent and out the other door. In a moment he returned with an armful of urine bottles and handed them out around the ward. "Don't any you guys break these things. That's a brand new cement floor and it'll stink for weeks. And don't try filling them up to the brim. Well, now everybody's cozy, my name's Valentine. We call this town Carentan, U.S.A., just so you won't get homesick. I'll be the ward boy in here, in the daytime. At night you'll be on your own, so anything you want, think of it before I go off duty. The guy that was supposed to be here, he went over the hill, no good bastard. First, I've got a direct order from the Colonel—any guns, knives, pistols, hand grenades, stilettos, switch-blades, bows and arrows—hand them over." He waited but no one made a move to offer him anything. "Of course, anything you got that I don't see—I don't blame you. Sorry nobody was here when you came. The other guy, he took off over the hill."

One of the men asked, "What's doing around this neck of the woods?"

"Well, down the road there, there's a few cafes. I guess all their women from around here took off to Paris. But you can get some of that apple whisky. I'd rather drink hospital stuff, myself."

One of the men bobbed up in bed, "Calvados? I ain't drunk none of that since way last summer. Boy! That's as hot as gasoline!"

"Yeah. It ain't anything but plain alcohol," Valentine said. "I prefer our own hospital stuff, cut with grapefruit juice. That's probably what happened to the other ward boy, got stewed. He don't often drink, but it don't pay you to give firewater to a redskin."

"He's an Indian?"

"Yeah. Name's Prancing Hoof. We call him 'Hoof,' around here. His old man's a chief somewheres out West, supposed to have a lot of money. Said he was in medical school when the war broke out. Most likely flunked out. We got him from a replacement depot in England. This hospital just came over from England three months ago. Hoof, he usually don't say much to nobody, but the French don't know it's against the law to sell a drink to an Indian. The other night Hoof hit a fellow, one of the patients. Oh, Hoof don't mean nothing by it. He gets that look in his face and he wouldn't know what he's doing. Everybody in his family, he told me, they get a government check once a year for fifty-two cents from a treaty they signed, a penny a week, if they haven't scalped nobody. Hoof won't get it for this year if he don't watch it."

"I'm glad as hell we don't have him!"

"Oh, Hoof wouldn't ever mean anything by it. Most of the time he'll practically eat out of your hand, but lately he's been acting like he was starting to turn wild. It's the patients, mostly. Hoof just can't get used to the patients. The other night a bunch of guys started kidding him about being in a hospital outfit, and him being so big. Said he was yellow. Hoof got mad, and I guess they got scared. One of them had a German pistol in the bandage around his chest and pulled it on him. Well, you know Hoof. All he had to do was see that thing pointing at him and he'd forget all about what came next. Hit that fellow so hard they had to take him in surgery and sew him up again. We never did see Hoof no more until morning. Came in yelling down the road on a horse, drunk. Stole it out of some barn. They got him quiet finally and the Colonel talked to him. We got a good Commandant over this hospital, all you have to do is stay out of trouble, and anything else is O.K. Said he was going to punish Hoof and the other guy, and transfer Hoof out. They had decided to put him in here for the time being, since this ward is only going to be half full."

"Not while we're in here."

"Me, neither."

"Of course, I know you're all combat men, but if you got anything on you, don't let anybody see it, or you'll get me in trouble. The Colonel's already had me up once this week. I'd like to keep out of his way. It was for going down in the town with some aspirins—they'll buy every one you bring. Well, I got to go see about your breakfast. Hoof was supposed to do that. I guess there's no use looking for him."

When Valentine was gone, a German pistol appeared out of a bathrobe pocket. "A guy like that might kill somebody."

And another German pistol. "Well, we're old buddy-buddy with Valentine. I wonder what they'll have around here for Christmas."

They sat polishing their pistols against their blankets.

"If that don't beat all, a redskin on the warpath, all the way over here in France."

"Oh, you'll find every damn thing in the army."

"These outfits in the Rear have to take what they can get."

"Maybe Valentine'll bring us some of that hospital stuff he drinks. It'd be nice for a change to drink something and know what it is."

"You know, it's going to get cold in here during the nights, and we might just need a little something now and then."

They realized that the tent was cold, and the four of them covered themselves up in their blankets.

Ross envied the Indian. He remembered when a gun had been pointed at him, how he had just stood there waiting to get it in the back, as though he were guilty of something and deserved to die. Guilty of what—of being a Negro? He wished now he had hit back like a man, the way the Indian had. He wished he had taken that rifle and beaten the guard with it. Maybe he had always thought he would die that way. Growing up in a black neighborhood, he had never known the day nor the hour.

The door opened. Another patient was brought in. It was Ed Webb.

# X

"HEY, ED! Where you been?"

"Yeah, Ed, we thought we had lost you."

"Aw—those Germans tried to take me away from my shipment and put me in where everybody had something like measles. They knew they hadn't ought to done that."

The men roared and Webb was placed in a bed. The door of the tent opened again. It was the nurse.

The men whistled and cheered.

She sounded off right back at them, "All right, knock it off! Where do you think you are? The Captain is coming to have a look at your feet, so make up those beds."

Webb said, "But we're in them."

"Fold them down neat, and leave your feet sticking out."

Webb said, "You don't have to eat us out, lady."

"Lieutenant," she told him.

"Lieutenant. We ain't done nothing—yet. I was just this minute thinking—"

"Well, don't sit there thinking. Make up those beds. And give me all hospital tags. All tags."

She proceeded to collect them and write bed numbers on them.

Ed Webb said, "You going to be here all the time, ma'am?"

"Yeah. You got any argument?"

"Naw. It's just you come in here chewing us out about nothing, and don't even tell us your name."

"Beulah."

"Well, now! That's a right pretty Southern name."

"New Hampshire."

"Oh." Webb looked at her uniform. "How come you gals way back here have to wear pants and helmets? In Paris they didn't wear nothing like that."

Beulah laughed. "I'm going to tell you something so you'll know. You're in the Rear. Get it through your heads. Back here we make formation. You'll march when you're well enough to go to the mess hall. Some of you guys can walk. You don't fool me. Don't let me see you on your feet, or I'll bring you your clothes. And when you start rambling all over that village, just be sure I know where you are. Now stay put. I got to take temperatures."

Most of them had been off their feet for over a month. It was the only treatment, except for the sulfa drugs when they first came in. They had been allowed to do anything but walk, or wash their feet, and for most of them the swelling had gone down. Before they left Paris, some of them had walked, but Ross hadn't tried.

When the captain made his rounds, he listened to the pulse in each foot, and for some of the men that artery had begun to function with the same pace as the heart. In the worst cases, men like Shanahan, who had been flown back to the States, the pressure of the swelling had been too much. Blood had spilled out of the veins into the flesh. There was nothing to do then but amputate.

When the doctor came in, he asked one or two of the men to stand, and when they said they could not, he made a speech about the USO shows, the movies, and the Red Cross center where they could go and make leather wallets and watch straps; then he and the nurse left the tent.

The men were silent for a long while, and then they began all talking at once.

"Well, that done it!"

"Looks like this is the end of the line."

"And it don't cost nothing to ride back."

Ed Webb said, "Damn if they're going to rush me out of here. I'm just getting interested. If they start getting ideas about me, I'll go out there at night and stand in the snow."

"Yeah, you hear all that crap about leather wallets and watch straps?"

Webb said, "I'm for everybody staying in bed, and when you got to piss, hold it till they bring you a duck, even if it's all day."

The nurse came back, followed by Valentine and a German carrying a long thermos box between them. Beulah called out, "O.K., boys, come and get it!"

Two men threw back their blankets to get up, then sheepishly got back in bed.

Beulah was amused. "Uh-huh. I thought I'd catch you. I don't know what you did in Paris, but you won't get away with anything here. This hospital is getting crowded, and the Captain doesn't mind making room."

Valentine and the German opened up the thermos box and Beulah began to spoon up ham and sunnyside-up eggs. She said to Ross, "How many can you eat, Paul?"

He was startled to hear his name. She had read his tag.

She handed him a plastic tray. "Now, let's see what you can do with that."

Valentine was not as careful. He tore the fried eggs with the spoon, and he dropped a slice of ham on the cement floor.

Ed Webb got his tray from the German. "Didn't nobody ask me what I could eat. He ain't the only soldier in this war. Didn't nobody ask me nothing."

The nurse was busy at her desk and didn't hear him.

Ed Webb said, "You got to be a big brave hero to get something out of these people in the Rear."

Beulah bristled. "Something wrong with your chow, soldier?"

"No, ma'am!"

Beulah went back to her work.

"Chow, soldier," Ed Webb said. "Son of a bitch."

Beulah stood up. "Let me tell all of you something. I don't want to hear any of that cursing and swearing around here, any more. You hear? I told you before, where you are. This is the Rear, whether you like it or not, and I'll have the respect you were taught to give an army officer, or I'll know the reason why! That's right, I'm throwing my rank, because it just isn't in any of you to have any courtesy for a woman! If you want to get rough, they've got a place for all of you up at the Front!"

"Son of a—"

"All right! Just try me! You think I like this? If you weren't so hard up for somebody to nurse you, I wouldn't be here! I'd be back in the States, getting some fun out of life!"

The men began to clap their hands and cheer, except for Ross. She glanced at him and stalked out of the tent. As soon as she was gone, Ed Webb yelled out as loud as he could, "Son of a bitch!"

"My heart bleeds for her," said another, and they all laughed.

Ross stopped chewing and got the attention of the German, and motioned for the big kitchen knife, to cut his ham.

"I'm not going to like anything about this place," Ed Webb said. "I'd be better off back with my outfit."

"I reckon that's the general idea," another said.

When the German went around to collect the trays, the kitchen knife was not on Ross' tray, and nowhere else that the German could see. He waited for Ross to give it to him, but Ross ignored him, so he came to attention and walked stiffly away with the trays.

In the days that followed, some of them began to ask for clothes, and came back raving about the movies and the town. Actually, the town was dank and closed, except for one or two bars, and there they stood among farmers shivering in their overcoats, drinking calvados. But Ross did not leave his bed. He sat watching Ed Webb, no one else. And he listened to every word he said.

"The best break I ever saw a fellow get was when we were street-fighting in front of a bunch of stores. A buddy of mine named Houston Magee, from Charlottesville, Virginia, was going along with a grease gun just shooting the hell out of anything that moved, and whatever hit him knocked out the whole plate glass window behind him. Magee was hit good but something made him reach on in there, in the store window, and grab him a fur coat, and he never let go of it. After the medics fixed him up, he told me it was a genuine fur coat, worth maybe two thousand dollars, and when they put him on the plane to go home, he still had it over him. Said he was going to give it to his wife."

Day after day was the same. Webb talked to the men, and Ross listened. It was like a drug, small doses but often, and given directly into the vein. Ross had succeeded in getting away from his company; yet here he found no way to avoid being continuously bathed in the same malignant infection—unless he decided to take the kitchen knife and empty Ed Webb's guts out on the floor. But not yet. He listened to Ed Webb.

"Naw, you Yankee boys can't make me mad talking like that, because you don't know what you're talking about. Called yourself emancipating the niggers. You stole everything that wasn't nailed down! After this war, you wouldn't do Germany the way you did the South! You wouldn't even do the Japs the way you did the South! All of that wasn't on account of no niggers. Didn't anybody need all those niggers, and don't nobody want them now. We could have told you that wasn't no way to run a civilized country. We were engaged in a great civil war, to see if this nation or any other nation so conceived and so dedicated, could break right across the middle, your half living off my half. But one of these times that's all going to come back at you. You can't run a country on a pack of lies, about the South or about anything else, because a lie can eat a country down like quicklime can eat a man! I'm not proud. As far as that goes, there ain't any more ill-treated, cheated, stolen-from, took-advantage-of minority in the whole United States than the Southern white man!"

That afternoon Ed Webb stopped talking. Like a man preparing for a secret mission, he went around the tent collecting the emergency combat D rations from the pistol belt of each man who had been given his clothes. Then he sat down and broke them all into small pieces with his pistol butt. Other patients began to help. They melted the rations in a steel helmet resting in a pan of water on the pot-bellied stove—added sugar stolen from the mess hall, fresh butter, and milk—and stood sweating, naked to the waist, each man taking his turn holding the hot helmet in the boiling water and stirring the mixture with a long spoon. Ross was puzzled by the operation; then he heard one of them mention that it was Christmas Eve. They were making a batch of fudge.

# XI

FOR ROSS, this night would be the nadir and *dénouement* of his life. His future would be clear, and therewith the future of the world. Now he was Jason, with only the dragon of self standing between him and the fleece. Whatever good he had sought within his blackness, he would now have to steal back from white men. It had been done before in his family.

That night Ross sat in his bed watching the others make a Christmas tree out of olive green army bath towels wrapped around a bunch of wire stuck in a can of dirt. They tore up bits of absorbent cotton all over it and cut out silver balls from chewing gum paper, blue ones from sulfa tablet cartons, red ones out of paper and mercurochrome. Then they cut up a cellophane gas mask wrapper and made icicles. Two sheets from a prescription pad and a pair of scissors, and they had a star.

The door of the tent opened and Ed Webb, in an overcoat, staggered in, carrying four bottles. One was half empty. He stopped short at the door and looked all around for the nurse, but she was gone. Then he began to sing, "*I sold my shoes, for a bottle of booze. . . . Nobody knows, I sold my shoes!*"

The men rushed over and caught him and his bottles.

before they fell on the floor. As they picked him up, he went on singing, "*I sold my clothes, for calvados. . . . Nobody knows, nobody knows . . . !*"

They carried him over to his bed.

"Ed, you ought to be on the radio."

"He's so loud, he don't need a radio."

"Where'd you get all the stuff, Ed?"

Ed Webb grinned and tried to sit up, "Sold m' clothes."

They looked inside his overcoat. He had nothing on underneath but a suit of underwear.

Ed Webb became indignant, "I just wanted everybody to know . . . a Rebel ain't no different . . . give you the clothes off his back . . . and it's the end of the line. Don't cost nothing to ride back." His eyes closed and he passed out.

One of them said, "If they hadn't a-gave us two pair of shoes, old Ed probably would have come walking in here barefoot."

None of them knew quite what to do next, whether to pick up a bottle and start drinking, or wait for Ed to sleep it off.

Ed shook himself and sat up. "Who's drunk? Who said I'm drunk?" He lay back and began to snore, but woke himself up with the noise of his own snoring. When he saw the bottles beside him and the men standing around, he tried to talk but the words were thick, "Don't. . . . Don't just. . . . Huh. . . . Don't just. . . ." He motioned toward the bottles and picked one up to pull the cork. "It's a long way back into combat, and everybody's got to have one for the road!"

They all laughed and started the bottles around, but Ross lay with his eyes shut.

One more drink sobered Ed so he could talk, "Tell Valentine to bring us a can of grapefruit juice so we can cut this T.N.T."

"Might kill it, Ed."

"Might make it blow up!"

Ed Webb beamed and picked up another bottle and bit out the cork. The men turned all the bottles up and drank long drinks of calvados, frowned and coughed.

Ed was back in voice. "Well, this is just about as cozy as sitting up guarding crops! Tell you who I met?"

"Tell it, Ed!"

"Go ahead, Ed!"

"Met a farmer, said he put manure on his strawberries. Told him I put sugar and cream on mine!"

They all laughed and drank and Ed began to sing, *"I am a rebel soldier, and that's just what I am. About the Constitution, I do not give a damn. I'm glad we fought against it. I only wish we'd won. I do not want no pardon for anything I've done!"*

The song was so splendidly in revolt, the others wanted to sing, but they didn't know the words.

*"I hate the Yankee nation, and everything they do, and the Declaration of Independence, too. I hate the nasty eagle, with all his brag and fuss! But the lying, thieving Yankees, I hate them wuss and wuss!"*

The men roared with delight. Ed had another drink, and sang on, *"Three hundred thousand Yankees are stiff in Southern dust. We got three hundred thousand before they conquered us. . . ."* Ed broke off and began to weep.

They were all too stunned at his weeping to know what to do. Then they began to pat him on the back, "It's all right, Ed. We all know where we're going when we leave out of here."

"Straight to hell," one said, and they all began to laugh.

Ed Webb laughed too and started again, ". . . *They died of Southern fever, and Southern shot and shell. I wish it was three million, that we had sent to hell! Ooooh, I can't take up my rifle and fight them now, no more, but I ain't a-going to love them, and that is certain sure. I do not beg no pardon for what I was AND AM! I won't be re-con-structed, and I DO NOT GIVE A DAMN! Eeeee-ya-HOOO!"*

They all answered back, *"Eeeee-ya-hooo!"* And then all drank.

"Sang another one, Ed!"

Ed sat wide-eyed, staring at the Christmas tree, and then he smiled, "Did I . . . did I ever tell you the one about the two niggers driving a jeep?"

"Tell it, Ed."

Ross held his breath. His hand slid under his pillow and gripped the handle of the kitchen knife.

"Well, the way it was told to me, seems they were . . . they. . . ." Ed passed out.

The men carried him to his bed, took off his overcoat, and covered him up. Then they didn't quite know what to do with themselves. They handed around what was left in the bottles and went to bed and smoked, then fell asleep. One soldier lay on his elbow for a while, feeling the shape of his new steel helmet, and then quietly he placed it down on the cement floor.

Long after midnight, when the tent was still, Ross opened his eyes and sat up, putting on his bathrobe. He tried to stand up. His feet did not hurt. The cement was cold and his knees were weak. He tied the bathrobe in front and looked around to see who was still awake; then his hand went under the pillow and brought out the knife. He sent it down into the pocket of his robe, ripping through the pocket until all of it was out of sight.

As he began to walk, he became dizzy. He bit his lip to keep going, and dragged himself along by the edge of the bed. At the end of his own bed, he stopped to decide whether it would wake the man in the next bed for him to support himself against it, and instead he crossed the aisle and grabbed the edge of the desk. He almost fell against the stove. He sat down in the chair to rest. It was farther than he had walked in a long time, and the floor was cold.

Then he stood up and gripped the edge of a bed and went from one to the next until he got to Ed Webb. They were all asleep. It was the calvados. Ed Webb was lying on his face. Ross stood with one hand in the bathrobe pocket on the handle of the knife. With his other hand he took Ed Webb's head by the hair and lifted it, "You, wake up!"

Ed Webb did not move.

"Soldier, wake up!"

He was not even breathing.

Ross shook the head, "What's the matter with you, soldier!"

A trickle of thick black vomit ran down from the side of Ed's mouth.

Ross slapped him, "What's the matter with you, soldier!"

The slap brought a rush of chocolate fudge vomit. Ed Webb whimpered once but could not get his breath.

Ross snatched the blanket off, and with both hands he pressed down on Ed Webb's back. He gave a long gagging belch and more of the vomit came, and then breath, but he could not inhale. He was dying, so now it would simply be a matter of watching it happen? No, he had to pull Ed Webb together—so he could kill him himself!

Ross took his bathrobe off and threw it on the floor. He wiped Ed Webb's face with his bed sheet and forced his mouth open. Ed's lower dental plate was loose in his mouth, and a partial upper plate was in his throat. He pulled them out; then he climbed on the bed and pressed on Ed's back, and up. Down. And up. He began to count. "One thousand-one,one thousand-two, one thousand-three. . . ." Air was going in and out of Ed's mouth, but not for long. His whole body would contort with violent vomiting. Ross had to start again. "One thousand-one, one thousand-two, one thousand-three. . . ."

After more than an hour, Ross was able to make him breathe for whole minutes before he went into dry heaves.

The night nurse looked in, "Oh, my Lord, what happened?"

Ross looked up, too exhausted to see her clearly, "He's drunk."

"I'll get some adrenaline." She darted out of the tent and came back with a hypo and some wet cotton. Ross stopped pumping to watch the muscles in his back while she gave the injection. The muscles continued unaided for a moment; then they stopped.

Ross was kneeling in chocolate and something like macaroni in the bed, and kept sliding into the wrong position. He could not keep up the rhythm and the pace much longer. He turned Ed Webb over on his back and began to slap his face with the palm and back of his hand. The head fell to one side and then the other. The hand swung out higher and higher and came crashing into the face until the fingers rang with pain and the flesh around the eyes began to bleed.

As though she were far off, Ross could hear the nurse screaming, "Stop! You'll kill him! Stop! Oh God, stop!" She grabbed Ross' arm, making him slide down on top of Ed Webb.

When they examined Ed, he was breathing.

Ross and the nurse took off Ed's underwear and all the bedclothes; then she brought sheets and blankets, and two pairs of pajamas. Ross changed into one pair, and then they remade the bed and changed Ed Webb. As she began to wash him, he urinated on the sheets and on her. They changed the bed and the pajamas again.

Just about sunrise Ross picked up his bathrobe and dragged himself back to bed. On his way he felt something in one of the pockets—the kitchen knife. He held on to the edge of a bed while he looked back at Ed Webb. He remembered the guard in the woods behind the service club, and he understood now how it was that he was alive. If that guard had come up against fear, he could have killed Ross.

When Beulah came in, she and the night nurse talked in earnest whispers, the night nurse waving her arms, and Beulah with her hands on her hips. Valentine and a German appeared at the door with the food box and a pot of coffee. Having slept through it all, the men dragged in and out the door, going to the latrine.

Valentine asked, "How many still eat on the ward? Two, or three? I forget." He served up ham, eggs, bread and coffee, and handed it to Ross.

Beulah said, "Just two, but save the coffee. I don't think some of them can make it to the mess hall this morning."

"Oh? What happened?"

"Drinking," Beulah said. "One of them almost died."

Valentine laughed, "Sold his clothes for calvados."

Beulah put her hands on her hips, "Valentine, were you in on this? So help me, I'll—"

"No, honest. They're all singing that, all over the hospital. Has the Captain been in?"

"No."

"Good thing."

Ed Webb began to stir. His lips fashioned the words to the song about shoes and booze, and the men burst out laughing. He raised himself on one elbow and felt around under the bed for a bottle, "I got to have my eye-opener."

Beulah was not amused.

One of the men said, "Yeah, Ed, let's go get us some."

Ed saw the nurse, "Calvados? I never touch the stuff."

Beulah said, "You're not funny. You know you almost killed yourself last night?"

"Aw—what did I do now?" He felt his face, "Oooo—! What the goddamn hell did I do?"

Beulah was ready to blow up. "You got pickled! That's what you did! Where are your clothes?"

Ed Webb poked around on the bed, "Somebody must have taken them out to get dry cleaned."

The men giggled and Beulah stomped her foot, "I'm going to get you the hell out of here! That's what I'm going to do! If you can't walk, you'd better learn fast!"

"Aw—it ain't no need of you taking on like that, just because we had us a little Christmas."

"Do you know they worked on you for four hours last night? You wouldn't even be alive this morning if that colored boy hadn't saved your life!" She pointed at Ross.

Ed looked all around the tent and then over at Ross. He shook his head unbelieving, "Him a nigger—?"

Beulah gasped. Valentine dropped a fork, and it bounced and rang on the cement floor until it was still. Ed Webb and Ross sat looking at each other, then both lay back down on their beds. Ross was surprised that the epithet did not hurt him. It seemed that for the moment nothing could hurt, which was a waste, for there must have been times when such an immunity could have been put to better use. And he remembered Tillie. . . . Tillie running down the hill . . . pretty Tillie running down the hill with something wrapped in paper in her hand. . . . Her smile turned to bewilderment at the way Ross was coming toward her. Tillie running down the hill, holding the pig embryo from the biology laboratory, holding it up *to show it to him,* but he ran right into it against his face . . . and he walked on.

She yelled after him, "I didn't mean it! I didn't mean it, crazy boy!" But was she laughing or crying?

Ross did not dare look back to know.

Valentine came over to Ross and found him crying. "Don't pay any attention to what Ed said. He thinks he's funny."

Ross could not stop crying. He buried his face in the pillow and sobbed, *"Tillie . . . Tillie loved me."*

Beulah said, "You ought to get a medal for what you did."

## *Integration*

## *XII*

Ross DID not get a medal, though at a practical level something unyielding had relented. He had been segregated, and desegregated, not from one race or another but from his humanity. It would have been no different whatever the color of his skin. However long in coming, he now had something of his own, not a cure entirely, but a clue. It was small and elusive, but in an empty wallet it was something to carry.

Wednesday evening, the third of January, Valentine called the roll and they bundled up in new overcoats and steel helmets, grabbed their duffel bags, and went out to get in the trucks. About a thousand in all, they rode through town to the railroad station with the hospital commandant in a jeep behind them.

Ross climbed into a boxcar where a handful of men had already moved in. One was sitting on a seat cushion from the first-class train on the next track, tuning a guitar, with a bottle of calvados beside him on the floor. Another was opening a can of bacon with a bayonet, and two more, with fire axe and crowbar, were tearing a plank out of the wall of the boxcar to feed a fire already going in the middle of the floor.

As the train began to pull away, the old colonel stood up in his jeep. "Goodbye, boys! Good luck! Goodbye, Hoof! Give 'em hell!"

They closed the boxcar door halfway, and settled down on the floor around the fire. Every man gave his letters, magazines and books to feed the flame, but no one was allowed to burn twenty-seven rolls of toilet paper that were collected and placed by the door. The sound of the axe was heard late into the night.

Out the door, the moon lit a changing pattern of splintered forest and battered village, of cemeteries from other wars, crusted in the dignity of untrodden snow—men plowed under, cross behind cross and star of David, dressed off and covered down in eternal formation. The men on the train sang a hymn, and the guitar joined in, *Rock of ages, cleft for me. . . . Let me hide myself in Thee. . . .*

By the third night they all had diarrhea. And they took turns hanging out the boxcar door with their pants down. The problem was not to fall.

One night a British fighter pilot looked down and saw a column of equally-spaced flames moving along a railroad track behind the lines, cursed, and made a pass at full throttle. The fires were trampled out and they slept cold, so cold they clenched their teeth until their jaws ached. But after a week they got off at Fontainbleau and went in trucks to the chateau—a bath, a hot meal, and a rifle. Then they moved on, riding on seats now, with a pot-bellied stove in every car, together with clean, young replacements just arrived from the States, to a rest area just behind the Front, whether in France or in Belgium, no one seemed to know.

And then big-head Finley drove in, asking for Ross. They were in Luxembourg, Finley told him. And just about the time Ross was being moved from Paris to Carentan, the order had come down for the 49th Salvage to prepare its heavy equipment for demolition and hold the road to the

Moselle. With cleaned rifles they spent that night on the hill across the road from their chateau. The following day the order was rescinded.

As for Christmas Eve, the company had marched from the chateau into a dismal, abandoned, nearby town to be shown a movie by Sergeant Neal. While the men were inside, the theater was bombed, and back at the chateau their trailers and equipment were strafed. There were no casualties, but the peculiar circumstances led to an army investigation of the 49th Salvage.

It was revealed that five civilians being quartered and fed by the company were collaborationists signaling German aircraft.

The company had moved twice since the chateau on the Moselle. When Ross and Finley caught up, it was in Longuyon, about to move again, somewhere between Arlon and Bastogne.

Then it moved into Germany—Wittlich, Wiesbaden, town after town still burning when they arrived. And they were finding themselves unable to do even a week's work, else they were too far behind the lines. In Würzburg, and in Nürnberg, the trucks were not even unloaded.

By late spring, fueling up to move on to Pilsen, the 49th was ordered back to France to be equipped and shipped to the Pacific. That August, going by train to the port of Marseille, they were flagged to a stop on the railroad bridge at Avignon—the war in the Pacific was over.

There was now set in motion a plan to desegregate the army—finally, one in every other foxhole.

There was nothing more simply done—like chess pieces they were moved into each other's squares. Most of the 49th went to companies doing occupation duty in Germany. As a college student, Ross was quickly assigned to a desegregated company running a documents and records depot about sixty miles from Paris.

It was a dull job. The actual work was done by a staff of French government clerks and stenographers who all fled to Paris on weekends. As for the desegregation, the subject seldom came up. The races were never mentioned as though none were permitted to exist. As for the French, they began to offend certain army personnel by referring to them as *les noirs,* or the even more offensive sounding *les nègres.* Dictionaries were brought into the matter and it was quietly made known that no offense would be found in *les hommes de couleur,* which the French carefully used for a while and then shortened to *les colored-guys,* about which no one complained.

The subject also came up in long, beery discussions with one white guy who went around with the colored guys insisting that he was simply not aware of the color of people. Ross did not believe him, but understood him. The whole subject was like some widely-held superstition. If you grew up being careful about not walking under a ladder, and being scolded if you did, finally you would have to start doing it every chance you got, just to prove—to the ladder, at least—that nothing would happen. Ross told the guy to go ahead and be white, and let black people be black, and maybe they could talk to each other about that, but he never understood what Ross was saying. And then there was the old guy, Willie, in the motor pool, who took care of the garbage cans, for whom the desegregation seemed to mean that he had to be angry all the time, or clowning, or some kind of Casanova to the older French women. Beyond that, Ross could see no one giving much to desegregation, not from any unwillingness, but simply from not knowing how. For him it was almost as though he had been here before and knew what should be, or almost knew. With the war over, he planned to get back into college and study the subject—was it sociology? Psychology? Or was it all of civilization?

While at the documents and records depot, Ross received a letter from Gary. Roscoe had lost a leg and Skin had been killed by an antitank mine while guarding prisoners. The mine field had been cleared and used all summer for baseball, but with the change in the weather they and the prisoners were huddled around a fire they had built on the ground, over a mine. Gary had lost his nose.

After answering Gary's letter, Ross wrote down Skin's story of the slave, Nicodemus:

### NICODEMUS

#### AS TOLD BY PVT. JAMES BUTLER, DECEASED

Those boats that used to go over to Africa and buy colored people—well, it came a time when things got hard up from people thinking about catching folks to sell to the boats, instead of thinking about growing something in the ground. And then things got so bad, people started saying, "We better sell up some of our own." But it was one fellow, he had told them, a long time ago, that they was going to get short doing what they was doing, cause it made them where they didn't put their mind to growing something in the ground. And he heard that they were going to start selling their own people, and he come and said, "How come you don't quit all this way of doing, and go head on and put some sweet potatoes in the ground, and all such as that, like colored folks spose to do?" But you see, he was talking like that to his own daddy, because it was his own daddy, was the Chief. So his daddy say, "Boy, you don't be talking to your own daddy like that. And anyway, this here ground is hexed where it won't grow nothing, cause of the Blind Man in the swamp."

The Blind Man, he was somebody could put a hex on you, and if you didn't know about something, he'd explain you. Well, all the people, they said the same thing. They said, "Boy, you don't be talking to your own daddy like that. You don't know about it. You ain't never been hungry, cause you is the Chief's boy, and you got gold rings on all your fingers, and in your nose, and in your ears, and bracelets around your hands and your feet. You is almost as fat as your daddy. How you know what has to be done?" So he commenced to thinking about it, all those young people he had grown up with, was going to get sold when the boat came, and he went off by himself until he came to the Blind

Man in the swamp and he said, "Mr. Blind Man, what I'm going to do about this?" And the Blind Man, he said, "Boy, I don't believe you going do nothing about it. Ain't you the Chief's boy? Ain't you going to be the Chief when your daddy die?" The boy shook his head. "Well," said the Blind Man, "what you come to me? I don't speak to none of you all any more. You people have gone crazy in the head. You can just go to them white people's Blind Man to explain you things." And with that, the Blind Man went on back in the swamp to himself.

Well, that poor boy started wandering around in the woods. Didn't eat nothing. Slept on the ground. Even walked right into trees in the broad daylight. Then he got mad and pulled all the gold rings off his fingers and out his nose and ears, and took off all his bracelets and threw them down. Then he walked on some more and he took off all his clothes what the Chief's boy spose to wear and he throwed them down, too. Then he went and sat down on a hill. Now, you see, folks had told him it wasn't nothing to getting sold and put on the boat, cause where they be going, it would be plenty for them to eat and they were all going to have it good. But he didn't believe none of that, cause he believed it was a hex on their land cause folks didn't do nothing for all the time running out in the woods catching people to sell, and he figured it would be a hex where they be going, for all those white people coming all the way there, instead of staying home and growing what white people spose to grow in the ground.

Well, by and by, he looked out and he seen the boat coming, so he got up and went back down to town, and on the way he was studying about what he was going to do. And when the folks saw him coming, they said, "Boy, where you been all this time? What you do with your clothes? What's the matter with you?" But he didn't talk to nobody. He got his mind on all the young folks was being tied to a long chain to go on the boat, crying and begging folks not to make them go, and he walked over to where they was, and he see his old daddy being paid off by the man from the boat, and he say, "I hope you know what you did!" And his daddy say, "How come you act crazy like that? When I die, what people going to say when you the Chief? Go put on your clothes."

Well, the boy, he didn't say nothing back, but when the young folks started walking, he ran and took hold to the chain with them, and went right on up in the boat like it wasn't nothing to it. And then everybody got scared and didn't know what to do, and his daddy yell, "You got one more on the boat than you spose to! You got my boy up there on that boat!" But the man yell down to his daddy, "You better be quiet, now. I done paid you." And his daddy, he act like he was going to throw a spear at the man, and the man haul off and shot his old daddy in the stomach. And while he's laying there on the beach moaning and dying, the boat moved on off.

Then everybody on the boat got happy and commenced to say, "You ain't no more boy, now. You is the Chief!" But the white people, they got scared they were going to have trouble out of him, so they put chains on him all over, and they called him Nicodemus out of the Bible. And when the war came along, he was an old gray headed man by then, and he looked like he wasn't going to live to go free and have his chains took off, so when he died he said, "Don't put me in the ground. I wants to be put in a hollow tree where you can come wake me up when the good times roll!"

# *XIII*

Ross COULD remember when he would have said nothing was accomplished by what Nicodemus had done, certainly nothing to change the situation of being a slave. But now

Ross was changed. It was clear to him that the chief's son could have done nothing else, for the chief had put himself with the white man, and the son had put himself with his black brothers. It had been left to him only to find it within himself to do what he did, else to do less would have been, as the Blind Man had said, to do nothing.

What Ross had written as an exercise in memory suffered from having already become a legend. It lacked details he would have liked to know—exactly when and where it had taken place. Still it was a terrifying story, more than he had realized, for he had heard it too often, like Skin's story about the bottom pig—the nigger in the bunch.

One first impression Ross found that he had to correct was that Nicodemus was simply a story about black men against white men. Rather it was the just against the unjust, good against evil, and that could be black against black or white against white. In the depot Ross was known as black, without any question; his arrival had been clearly identified with the desegregation. Yet he found himself resisting the kind of conversation among blacks which whites could hear but not understand. It seemed that unless he was careful he might find himself alone with the French.

He had been restored to his military occupational specialty as a personnel clerk, and along with his forty files of the men in his detachment were some two hundred files of civilian employees. For the French who found work at the depot, life was far from prewar standards, but they did have three meals a day, soap, American cigarettes, vitamin pills, and medical care. It was better than working for the German army (nearly all of them had done that), which required their coming to work on time, always being properly dressed for the job and never showing any emotions day-after-day face-to-face with the Nazis. They had been polite to the Nazis—Ross could see that from the way they treated the American army.

Ross expected his number would come up soon for redeployment to the States. He was reluctant about that. Somewhere in the Halloween nightmare of war he had grasped a baffling inconsistency, something always rationalized into nonentity among the beery banalities and military obscenities. Yet he was sure it could change the world if he could have time to understand it. To prolong matters he had put in for a transfer so he could take a course being offered by the army in French civilization. He would be sent to Paris, but he saw it as no furlough; he intended to work seriously.

Meanwhile, he was kept busy with his files, long telephone conversations, public relations with the French police and answering official questions.

One Friday after supper he was on the telephone explaining about a French civilian employee, Jacques, the night watchman, who had hanged himself. "No," Ross was saying, "we had no idea—Yes, *of course* we knew he was a decorated veteran—a veteran of the Great War as well as this one—

"Someone had requisitioned six padlocks," Ross continued, "and was then redeployed. When the requisition came through, no one knew what the locks were for. The supply sergeant hung one on the mess hall door and forgot to give the old night watchman the key. So he came and asked if we were closing the depot. We told him no. He said we were lying. Of course, I can't say we will be here forever. But we did tell him he could stay as long as we do. We knew he couldn't walk a guard post because of his leg, but it was worth it to us to have someone sit around all night in the mess hall."

When Ross hung up the phone, the major told him, "Quit knocking yourself out. You got to get out of here in twenty minutes. You had supper?"

"Yeah. Major, you were saying, you heard some woman had slashed her wrist?"

"Late this afternoon," the major said. "One of them went in the motor pool and tried it—that Madame Bernard. We grabbed her in time, else we'd be in the middle of a dag-gone three-ring circus. The medics fixed her up. It didn't get spread around among the French, but this thing with the night watchman—we haven't been able to do anything else for two days!"

The major sat earnestly locking and unlocking his desk drawer until he became aware of Ross watching him; then he straightened himself and pulled at the papers on his desk, "I have your orders here somewhere. You don't have to report until Monday morning, so I made you out a weekend pass. If you get redeployed, I'll send you a wire. Now don't miss your bus."

"Thanks," Ross said. He folded his orders to fit in the pocket of his jacket, put on his overcoat, and picked up his duffel bag. "You don't have to send that telegram. I'd like to stay and finish that course before I go anywhere."

In front of the headquarters office, Ross put his duffel bag down on the sidewalk and stood waiting. Hébert, one of the mess hall boys, was already there, folding and refolding a large white handkerchief in his breast pocket. He had no overcoat, but he had on two sweaters.

*"Il n'marche pas?"* Hébert asked him.

*"Pas encore,* Hébert," Ross told him. They both looked at their watches. Hébert cursed and wandered back into the mess hall.

A weapons-carrier came past the mess hall in low gear and parked in front of Ross. The driver, Claude, stepped out and growled something at the gathering fog, then went into headquarters. Ross lifted his duffel bag over the tailgate and was about to climb in, when Thérèse came over and joined him.

"Hi! I see you got transferred to the Sorbonne," she said. "You will ride with us tonight, yes?"

"I guess nothing around here is a military secret."

"But I mimeographed your orders!" she laughed. "And just for that, we know more about your army than you do!"

They climbed into the weapons-carrier. There was room for eight, four on each side. Thérèse picked the left bench and moved into the corner. "Here, sit beside me," she said, "and keep me warm."

Ross joined her and she leaned on his shoulder. There was no question about it around the depot that Thérèse would marry an American, definitely not a Frenchman. She said so herself. Many of the girls said that they were disillusioned with French men because of the German occupation, and they seemed equally cautious about American white guys.

"This morning," she said, "Monsieur de Bonfons announced next week there are coming those colored guys who sing on Radio Paris, Les Harmonistes Spirituels."

"Yes, they're good," Ross said.

"I hear them on the radio," she said. "I like very much that song, *'Nous escaladons l'echelle de Jacob.'*"

"We are climbing Jacob's ladder," Ross said.

"Yes, do you know, *'Marchez dans l'eau'?*"

" *'Marchez dans l'eau'?*"

She sang the first line for him, *"Marchez dans l'eau, mes enfants!"*

"Wade in the water," he said.

"Yes, *c'est formidable!* Explain to me something, Paul. You would know—about this suicide."

"I don't know what I can tell you," he said.

"Old Jacques, the watchman—"

"He got the idea we were closing the depot. We will obviously close it someday. The war's been over for months."

She changed the subject. "I have never seen you with your decoration on your *veston*—your Eisenhower jacket. You have many."

"Those aren't decorations, Thérèse. That's what everybody got."

Monsieur Bercy looked into the weapons-carrier, "Monsieur, will you to help my wife into this automobile?"

Ross got up and took Madame Bercy's hand. It was a large hand, larger than his own, and the grip was painful. He had often seen her in the office, but she had never spoken, like many of them, trying to hide their poor English by using it seldom.

"Thank you, monsieur," her husband said to him. He continued in English, making it evident that this was a language he could command. "I think I too will sit in the corner."

Madame Bercy sat down on the bench, facing Thérèse. Monsieur Bercy stood tightening his scarf to get his wife to understand that he wanted the corner without his having to speak French. Finally he elbowed her up and they exchanged places.

Thérèse attempted to make conversation, "Yes, monsieur, I think it will be much more warm in the corner."

Monsieur Bercy beamed gratefully at Thérèse, "Since the war I am having to make attention to currents of air." He looked cautiously at Ross, "Why you are—ride with us, monsieur, instead of the army?"

Thérèse answered. "He is transferred from the depot to study at the University of Paris."

Monsieur Bercy was relieved. He made gay gestures, "A student at the University!"

"It's just a two-week course in French civilization," Ross told him.

Monsieur de Bonfons arrived from the mess hall and placed a silver-headed ebony cane on the bench beside Madame Bercy. As he climbed into the weapons-carrier he said to Ross, *"Vous avez pris ma place, monsieur."*

Ross could not imagine that he was serious, which annoyed de Bonfons and he began to speak in impeccable English, "My place, sir. You have taken my place!"

Ross stood up and let de Bonfons have the seat next to Thérèse. "Who's over here?" he asked her, pointing to the place beside Madame Bercy.

"I believe that is Mademoiselle Flaunet," she told him.

"I'm not going through that, again," Ross said, and he sat down on his duffel bag, between Thérèse and Monsieur Bercy.

Monsieur and Madame Bercy reached across him and shook hands good-evening with Monsieur de Bonfons, who asked them in French, in a low whisper, "Why do we have this protection tonight?"

Monsieur Bercy explained in English, "He is transfer to the Sorbonne, two weeks to study *la civilisation française.*"

*"Two weeks!* These Americans," de Bonfons grunted. He turned to Ross, "But my dear young man, you would need ten years, not two weeks."

Thérèse explained, "It's just a little scholarship of the French government, for the American guys to have in gratitude for the Liberation."

De Bonfons grunted something about *"l'Administration,"* and Monsieur Bercy whispered a translation to his wife.

Yvette arrived and climbed aboard. Ross got up to help her, but she pulled away from him and sat down beside Madame Bercy. She wore a metal brace from her shoulders to her hips, which held her stiffly at attention to her typewriter, but she would never permit anyone to assist her with anything. Among themselves the men in the detachment called her "The Girl Scout," referring to her brusque manner, *and* the fact that one of them discovered—without saying how—that she wore an above-the-knee sheath and commando knife with a brass-knuckle handle. She was a friend of Madame Bernard, who had attempted to kill herself. At least, they always argued a lot. Ross never heard what it was they argued about, except that he had heard Yvette call Madame Bernard irresponsible.

Hébert helped his sister, Mademoiselle Flaunet, into the weapons-carrier. Yvette was sitting in Mademoiselle Flaunet's place, but rather than have words about it, she and Hébert sat next to Monsieur de Bonfons.

The chauffeur, Claude, walked up and looked in. *"Alors, bonsoir messieurs 'dames,"* he growled.

Monsieur de Bonfons drew out his watch, "It is already past 7:10. Why are we still here?"

Monsieur Bercy looked at his wrist watch, "Yes, I have the same."

The driver growled at them, "You think I am the railroad, *heh?* I am not the railroad. If I am the railroad, I go away at 7:10, before *anyone* come but that American boy! There is still one place, and I go smoke a cigarette!" With that he went around to the front and sat behind the steering wheel.

Monsieur de Bonfons looked at the empty place at the end of the bench beside Yvette. "And who is missing?" he asked. "Monsieur and Madame Bercy, Mademoiselle Flaunet—"

"Madame Bernard," Yvette told him.

"Madame Bernard," he grunted, as if so what.

"Madame Bernard is late," Yvette announced.

Mademoiselle Flaunet snarled, "Oh, Madame Bernard—I would like to shave her head!"

Just then they heard her laughing, Madame Bernard. She continued to laugh, speaking bits of French and English, until she appeared, supported by the motor pool Casanova, Willie, who was telling her a joke. They had both been drinking. He helped her climb into the weapons-carrier.

"Good-bye, Willie! *Bon weekend!*" She sat down, then got up to reach for Willie, "Let me kiss you!" Claude started the motor, and as they moved away she kissed him, lost her balance, and began laughing again. Willie pushed her into the seat and waved good-bye.

Madame Bernard waved at him, "*Bon weekend, Willie! Bon weekend!*"

Monsieur de Bonfons drew out his watch, scowled, and put it back in his pocket. Monsieur Bercy looked at his watch, and for a while they all rode in silence.

Ross had heard remarks about Madame Bernard, that she had collaborated with the Germans. He found that hard to believe, and doubted that anyone at the depot knew the first thing about her. He had never been able to make much sense out of her file—where she had worked, and what she had done. She was a Jew, with the maiden name of Pollac, and she was a widow. She spoke English well, and German as easily as French. The depot had been only too glad to hire her without many questions. She had worked for the Germans, but then they had all worked for the Germans, just as now they all worked for the Americans—and looked it. Madame Bernard wore an old fur coat and American army boots; Yvette, a coat made from an army blanket; while the rest of them sported combat jackets, army gloves and officer's trousers dyed a darker color.

Now that the war was over, life would become harder before anything changed for the better. Ross thought of the story of Nicodemus and wondered how it applied. What Skin seemed to be saying was that you determine what is the chain in any situation, and you take hold of it. He tried to imagine a chief's son, safe from it all, reaching down and taking hold of a chain with slaves tied to it, and holding on while the chain was being pulled into the boat. . . .

Thérèse burst out laughing. "You should see the expression on your face," she told him. "Don't you want to go to Paris?"

"I was thinking of something else," he said.

Monsieur de Bonfons touched Ross on the knee and said, "Not a pretty thing, war." He smiled, "I am an old man, you see. I forget now precisely what day it was. It was during the Liberation of Paris. I was standing in a queue in Montmartre, with some women waiting to buy milk, and then this thing came along. I don't know the English word—like a tank, with the same sort of runners underneath, but open at the top, with five or six Germans standing up with shooters pointed in every direction." He held his cane up like a rifle. "And they rode slowly by us, pointing the shooters at us. The women began to scream and fall back against the building. I said to them, 'What is the matter with you! Can't they see you are only waiting to buy milk for your children? Don't budge!' I snapped it at them the way an officer gives an order, *'Ne bougez pas!'* And they quieted down and the Germans drove on. Certainly, if they had continued to scream at the top of their lungs, they would have been shot."

Yvette had ignored the story, Madame Bernard had drowsed, but the rest had been attentive. Mademoiselle

Flaunet said, "Oh, they would break your feet, those queues! The stores would open at five o'clock in the evening, but when we found out there would be not enough for everyone we decided to come the next day at a quarter to five. But someone was already there, so the next day we decided to come at a quarter past four. Being Parisians, everyone thought of that. Then we were coming at three o'clock, then two, then noon, until we were there in line at eight o'clock in the morning for stores that did not open until five in the evening! Why did they not all *decide* to come at five o'clock?"

Thérèse said to Monsieur de Bonfons, "I think that must have been the second day of the Liberation of Paris. They had told us not to come back to the office until it was over. I remember it was a very beautiful day and I could not hear anything happening in the streets, so I didn't want anyone to think I would use it for an excuse not to come to work on *such* a beautiful day, so I got dressed and went out very early because it was such a nice weather to walk. When I was three blocks from the office I met this same thing coming in the street as you said, with the Germans with machine guns. I was afraid to go back, so I went to the office as fast as I could. Just as I turned the corner I met a sixteen-year-old boy leaning against the building. He had a machine gun too! He looked so hungry and dirty! He said to me, 'Look the other way and keep going!' I was so frightened I turned my ankle, and when I got to the office, it was closed."

Monsieur Bercy touched Ross on the knee, "One did not know what to do. People were shot at random, without reason."

Hébert asked Ross, "Have you heard of some place in Normandie where we made resistance to the American soldiers because of the way the houses were bombed?"

Monsieur de Bonfons stopped him, "*Assez, Hébert!*"

"But I have heard this! I want to know."

"*Oh, dit donc, Hébert,*" Mademoiselle Flaunet said, "*pas d'histoire!*" And her brother was quiet.

They rode in silence, again. They seldom spoke of the war. When they did, no one ever spoke of events before the days of the Liberation. Ross had watched Yvette turn and look at Monsieur de Bonfons when he said, *"Ne bougez pas!"* as though she thought he was comical. It would have been hard to imagine Yvette in a war. She was pretty, in an intense way that made you think of something fragile that had been hidden away for years in a vault.

Just then, the wheels of the weapon-carrier screamed along the wet pavement. Ross was thrown against Thérèse, with Monsieur Bercy on top of him. They came to a dizzy halt off the edge of the road.

Claude shouted back at them, *"Asseyez! Asseyez!"* He threw the gears into reverse and backed the weapons-carrier into the road.

Yvette screamed. Madame Bernard's seat was empty.

Ross banged furiously on the wall behind him, "Stop! Stop, Claude!"

Claude let the weapons-carrier roll back into the shoulder of the road and threw on the brakes. No one moved for a moment; then quietly they began to push each other out into the fog.

Madame Bernard was lying on her back on the wet pavement. Ross knelt down beside her. She had a dirty bruise across her forehead from the fall, and a wheel print on her open coat into her blouse. She was conscious, though her eyes rolled without focus, and she whined softly between her teeth. Yvette stood crying, her hands pressed against her face.

Claude came around to them, "How could I know this? How could I know?"

"We'd better get her out of the middle of the road," Ross said, "before something else happens. Everybody help me pick her up."

They all reached under her and brought her evenly to the floor of the weapons-carrier. Then Ross asked Claude where they were. Claude did not know. "Then how far now to Paris?"

"Another forty kilometers."

"And back to the depot?" Thérèse asked.

"Sixty," Claude told her. "At least sixty."

Monsieur de Bonfons spoke up, "If you will permit me, I recall a very excellent sanitarium not three kilometers from here—a tubercular sanitarium. If I were permitted to ride with the chauffeur, we would find it. Everyone please resume his place so we may get on."

The rest climbed in with the miserable form of Madame Bernard on the floor at their feet. Claude yelled back for them to be careful, and they drove away.

Madame Bernard shrieked as they went over a lump in the road, and Claude slowed down, almost to a walk. Yvette was silent, involved in an agony of grief. Thérèse had Madame Bernard's pocketbook which she had picked up from the pavement. "These are villainous times for a thing like this, if you don't have insurance," she said, rumaging through the pocketbook. It was filled with bars of soap. Underneath there was a leather folder of identification papers.

Yvette reached over and grabbed the pocketbook away from Thérèse and stuffed everything back in it. Mademoiselle Flaunet hissed at Yvette and looked swiftly around the group for agreement, but Monsieur and Madame Bercy sat cowering in their corner as though at any moment they too would be tumbled to the pavement. Thérèse looked unconcerned. Yvette was without expression, as though the accident had never occurred. When Madame Bernard groaned with the movements of the weapons-carrier, Yvette did not even look at her; instead she kept her eyes on the ribbon of pavement that disappeared behind them into the fog.

Claude drove for some distance and stopped, turned around, and went in the other direction. Then he turned onto a dark private road and through a gate.

Monsieur de Bonfons got out and yelled back to them, "Quickly now, as we did before! Pick her up carefully and follow me!"

They all lifted Madame Bernard and followed him to where he stood holding a lighted door open with the point of his cane. Inside, under the light, was a receiving table where they put her down.

An old woman came into the room and stood wide-eyed, looking from one of them to the other. Monsieur de Bonfons bellowed at her, "Don't just stand there gaping! Go tell them we are here!"

She scampered out of the room, and Monsieur de Bonfons paced back and forth, drumming nervously first on a chair, then on a table. He turned to Ross, "You see, you must make a show of anger to get a thing done." As he turned around, there, looking at him from another door, was the old woman.

"Why are you waiting!" he bellowed. "Can't you see this is an emergency!"

She came trembling into the room, holding her apron, "*Mais, monsieur—! Monsieur—!*"

Monsieur de Bonfons thrust himself past her and stalked through the door and down the hall. They heard the even beat of his steps begin to slow, then stop, then running. From the far end of the building he called out, "Is there no one here!"

There was only silence.

Hébert began to laugh. Mademoiselle Flaunet slapped him hard across the mouth.

## XIV

MONSIEUR de Bonfons came back into the room, blinking at the light.

"Monsieur, they all left years ago," the old woman said.

"Then what are you doing here?" Monsieur de Bonfons demanded.

"I live here!" the old woman brayed at him.

Thérèse, always the girl Friday with the cool head, began looking around the room, "Maybe there are still medicines, after all—"

"Yes," Monsieur Bercy followed her. "We must give her something for the pain—some morphine!"

They went about the room and into adjoining rooms, opening cabinets and chests, pulling out drawers and examining closets. There was nothing they could use, only dust-covered bottles in which the contents had long since crystalized or decomposed, surgical instruments speckled with rust, pieces of rubber pipe crumbling into sticky gum, and medical files kept in German.

Ross said, "What we've got to find first is a doctor."

Monsieur de Bonfons bellowed at him, "And where do you propose to find one?"

"The army," Ross said. He turned to the woman, "Where is the telephone?"

She became almost contemptuous, except that she was amused, "But monsieur, it is years since there were telephones!"

"Then I'll go find one!" Ross yelled at her.

Like the rest, he'd about had enough of this old woman. As he started out of the building, Yvette followed after him, "Wait, monsieur! I will go with you!" She caught his arm and clung to it as they walked briskly down the driveway to the road.

"You are a friend of Madame Bernard?" he asked her.

She gasped at his understatement. "She is my idol!"

"Then why did she do what she did this afternoon?"

"How do you mean, monsieur?"

"You don't know?"

Yvette seemed not to have the slightest idea what he was talking about.

"She went out in the motor pool and slashed her wrist—tried to commit suicide."

Yvette moaned, *"No! Oh, no!"* She turned to go back, but Ross pulled her along with him, "What do they have against her?" he demanded.

"They are stupid!" Yvette growled.

"They seem to be very convinced about it," he said. "And you, you seem to be giving her hell about something every time I see you together."

"There are things you should not ask, monsieur," she told him and made it clear she had no concern for how he might accept that reply; then she broke into tears. They stood a moment while she wiped her eyes; then she said, "I think we will find a lighted house I saw when we were coming here," and they walked briskly on in silence, seeing nothing but the vague outline of the pavement beneath them and the faint glow of the fog.

Finally they stopped while Yvette peered through the fog for the lighted house. Far ahead they heard a car coming toward them and stood aside to let it pass. Then they were no longer sure in which direction it was coming. In the fog the sound of the motor echoed from all directions, nearer and nearer, until headlights burst through the fog directly at them. Yvette wrenched his arm back and threw Ross from the pavement. They fell together down an embankment, rolling among loose stones and wet leaves.

When Ross picked himself up, Yvette was standing over him. "Where did you learn judo?" he asked her.

"I learned it," she said, disapproving the question.

"Did you hurt yourself?"

"Oh, move along, monsieur!" she insisted, pulling him back up the embankment. Then, standing on the road, they saw what looked like the moon glowing through the fog, and ran toward it.

It was a lighted upstairs window in a house behind a stone wall. Ross shook the iron gate and a bell began to ring back and forth at the end of a coiled spring.

A darkened window opened in the attic. He called, "Hello!"

There was no answer.

Yvette began kicking the gate, making the bell ring, but no one answered. Then the lighted window opened and a woman leaned out. *"Qui est là?"*

Ross called to her, "We had an accident on the road, may we please use your telephone?"

The lighted window slammed shut, but after a moment the front door unlocked and opened, and the woman came out into the courtyard in her stocking feet and stepped into wooden shoes. "Ah, monsieur has had an accident in the road! These are villianous times!" She struggled furiously with a lock and chain that held the rusted gate. "A moment, monsieur. This old key—"

A figure leaned out of the darkened attic window and called, *"Qui est là?"*

"It's a monsieur who had an accident in the road, who wishes to use the telephone!" She turned to Ross and shook her head, "My poor sister, monsieur. She ran upstairs to hide the sausage and butter."

The lock fell to pieces in her hand.

The sister called down, "And how does the monsieur know we have the telephone?"

The woman thought a moment, then leaned her shoulder against the gate, waiting for Ross to reply.

"I didn't know," he said. "We saw the light and stopped to ask."

She turned to her sister, annoyed, "He didn't know! He saw the light and stopped to ask!" She opened the gate, "My poor sister, since the war—" She offered her hand, *"Bonsoir,* monsieur, madame. The telephone is in my bedroom. I will show you."

Ross and Yvette wiped their feet and followed her upstairs where she pointed to a knitted cover over a wooden instrument which resembled a telephone. The sister came to the bedroom door and watched their every move.

Ross picked up the receiver and listened. Nothing. Yvette explained that first he had to turn the crank. He turned it gently, afraid it would break; then Yvette tried it. He listened. Nothing. He picked up the whole thing and examined it, and one of the wires fell on the floor. Yvette picked it up and pushed it back in its slot and tightened the screw; then Ross held it firmly on the table and spun the crank.

Now there was a voice, but the words were not clear. "*Quel numèro appellez-vous?*"

He gave it to Yvette, "Tell her we want an American army hospital or a medical detachment—one that's around here."

Yvette took the phone, "*Allô! Allô! Répondez-moi!*" She handed it to the woman, "*La téléphoniste ne répond pas.*"

The woman held it firmly and shouted, "*Allô! Allô!*"

The operator asked again, "*Quel numéro voulez-vous?*"

Yvette took the receiver, "*S'il vous plaît—vite, le plus vite possible, donnez-moi le chef du bureau central! C'est un cas d'urgence—un accident—*"

The operator came back in a sing-song voice, "*Oui, madame, toute de suite. Il me faut l'appeller.*"

Yvette stomped her foot, "*Oui! Oui!—Faites-le vite!*"

Another operator came on, a man, "*Ici, le bureau central.*"

Yvette begged him, "*S'il vous plaît, donnez moi vite l'hôpital américain ou un détachment médical le plus près d'ici. C'est un cas d'urgence—*"

"*Oui, madame, c'est à Rheims,*" the operator replied.

"*Mais non, pas à Rheims,*" Yvette shouted. "*Ici! Ici!*"

"*Attendez une minute, madame,*" the operator told her. Yvette waited; then the operator said, "*J'ai un hôpital américain à Cherbourg—*"

"*Cherbourg—*" Yvette was furious, "*Ah! Comme même—non, non, pas à Cherbourg! Aux environs!* She turned to Ross in English, "These cretins! Name of god!"

The operator came back in English, "But madame, I do not have other American hospitals closer to here!"

Yvette roared at him, "*Alors*—a medical detachment, which there are, I am sure!"

The number was ringing. The operator asked, "You are willing to speak to no matter who?"

"*Bien sûr!*" Yvette shouted.

There was a voice on the line, "Twenty-Ninth Detachment, Corporal Taylor, Charge-of-Quarters, speaking." Yvette gave the telephone to Ross.

"Hello?"

"Twenty-Ninth Detachment, Corporal Taylor."

"Hello, Corporal? We've had an accident on the road, and we need an ambulance."

"A what?"

"*An ambulance!*"

"Man, we ain't got no ambulance."

"What outfit am I talking to?"

"Twenty-Ninth Detachment."

"Medical detachment?"

"Naw, this is the 29th Graves Registration Detachment. You got the wrong number."

"Wait a minute, Corporal! Look, our weapons-carrier skidded off the road and we've got a woman in a sanitarium here, but they haven't got a doctor!"

"We take our Sick Book all the way the hell to Cherbourg. Where are you?"

"What?"

"Where—are—you?"

Ross turned to Yvette, "Where are we? What's the name of this place?" As he turned, a wire pulled out of the receiver. They tried to poke it in, but this one had to be connected somewhere inside. They would have to take the whole thing apart.

"What will you do, now?" Yvette asked him.

"I'll go back and get the weapons-carrier, and we'll go find a doctor, even if we have to go all the way to Paris."

When they walked back to the sanitarium, Hébert and Mademoiselle Flaunet were sitting on the steps, smoking. Hébert asked Ross, "We go now?"

Ross walked past them without answering, and into the room. "The telephone went dead," he said.

"That's a pity," Monsieur de Bonfons said coldly.

In the light of the room they could all see that Ross and

Yvette were covered with mud and wet leaves. Thérèse burst into lewd laughter, "And what else were you two doing?"

"Perhaps what you think," Yvette snapped back at her and began to brush at Ross.

"We fell down," he said.

They all seemed no longer concerned about Madame Bernard, who was alert now, but obviously in pain. Ross wondered if the lack of concern had to do with the fact that in the depot personnel records she was listed as a Jew. Yvette pulled Madame Bernard's fur coat more closely around her and reached for her bandaged wrist, but Madame Bernard pulled it away from her and buried it inside the coat. Monsieur de Bonfons got up from his chair and put on his hat. "Then we are able to do nothing more here." As he started to leave, Monsieur Bercy made a move to follow him.

Ross told them, "I'm taking the weapons-carrier to go hunt for a doctor."

"But it's no use!" Monsieur Bercy shouted. "You don't know the region! None of us do. And some of us were to arrive at Paris at a certain hour."

Ross said, "That's an *American army* vehicle out there."

Monsieur Bercy reddened with anger and began to speak too fast for Ross to understand, "*Américain—! Qu'est-ce que ça vent dire? Où étiez vous en trente-neuf? Eh? Américain—! Qu'est-ce que ça vent dire? Que nous avons besoin d'une armée de jeunes chiens, de voyous, les bouches mouillées du lait de leur mères—pour nous libérer? Nous, nous les braves hommes de France, le berceau de liberté—d'une grande histoire que vous n'avez* jamais *approché—de soldats, de* vrais *soldats—la guerre de quatorze—la plus grande armée du monde!*"

If that was to insult Ross, it did not. It was somewhat of a delicious confusion to find himself called all of that, not for being black but for being an American. He suppressed a smile and asked them, "What was that all about?"

Like a secretary reading back her dictation, Thérèse told him, "He says: In 1914, the French army was the greatest army in the world."

Monsieur de Bonfons was about to speak, then waited until he had chosen his words carefully. "We needn't make a *comédie* of this. Of doctors, we know they exist—" He enumerated as though he were speaking to children. "—at the depot, and at Paris. Therefore—" His tone hardened into a command. "—it is logical that we proceed to Paris." Ross was ready to argue, but de Bonfons continued, *"Leaving someone here to attend her.* Then you, monsieur, can go to the American authorities for an ambulance." He paused. "Are we not all agreed?"

Thérèse, Mademoiselle Flaunet and Madame Bercy made it clear they were not volunteering. They got up to leave.

Yvette said, "I will stay."

"That is very excellent of you, mademoiselle," de Bonfons complimented her. "And make her to sleep for a while. Now let us waste no more time."

Yvette followed them all out to the weapons-carrier. As they climbed in, de Bonfons said to Ross, "Perhaps you should leave your possessions here—so you won't have to carry them around with you."

Yvette was shocked at the suggestion, "So he will be forced to return?"

With no hesitation, Ross pulled the duffel bag out of the weapons-carrier and heaved it as far as he could in the direction of the door of the sanitarium. He went to pick it up and carry it inside.

Yvette was right behind him, "No, no! They insult you! Take your bag!" she begged him.

Ross was too angry to respond, and dragged the duffel bag inside the door. When he came back out again to climb into the weapons-carrier, Yvette stopped him. Smoldering with indignation, she whispered to him, "Monsieur—I am—ashamed—of what he spoke to you! I will show them all—you will come back!" She put her arms around his neck and kissed him, then kissed him again.

Claude had come around to the back to look inside.

They were seated three on one side, and three on the other. He put his hands on his hips and sneered at them, "*Alors,* no one to sit at the end but the American boy?"

Monsieur de Bonfons was enraged, "Pay attention to your driving, you—! You—!"

"You pay attention," he growled at them. "So you don't fall on your head, *heh?*" Ross started to climb in but Claude stopped him, "No, you come—sit with me."

He sat in front with Claude and they drove off. "Ooooh, I would not do that kind of work they do!" Claude told him. "Government clerk! You heard what that one said to me, the cane—why didn't I leave at ten past seven o'clock—"

"Monsieur de Bonfons?"

"Heh. They do very well to be at the American depot, with a fleet of equipment. At Paris they can go to the railroad and take a chair and a book, and make crochet until the middle of the night like everybody else—what do I care?" He began a rumbling, coughing laugh. "When I came back from the captivity, all I had was my prisoner-of-war uni-*form.* Do you think they look at me? Ah, *non!* They gave us each, one thousand franc. We thought we had a lot of money. Before the war the most you could pay for the best drink was two franc, twenty-five centime. A coffee was only forty centime. And now for a wine is *twelve* franc! So why a woman would look at us? We didn't have anything. It was good to see the American come, and open our camp, but those people—" He pointed with his thumb behind him.

They drove a long while in silence; then Claude began again, "When you first came to our camp, we thought you were very funny look-*ing.* The English say, 'Yes, it is the American boys.' And we say, 'No, I don't think *so,*' and the English say, 'Oh, yes, it is American.' But we look out in the field and you all have on like a working man's clothes, instead of a uni-*form.* We never saw soldiers to look like that. You looked like house painters with the paint all over your clothes and face!"

"How long had you been a prisoner?" Ross asked him.

"Since the Retreat of 1939. —And then the German say, 'We are your prisoner.' And we say, 'But you are not our prisoner. We are *your* prisoner.' And they say, 'Yes, you are our prisoner, but we are your prisoner too, until the American come.' And we say, 'But how we do this?' And they say, 'Walk around. *Do what you want to do.*' And then we each made a flag of the country, for our liberation. And when we began to put them up, the Italians came out *with* a flag. So we say, 'No, you can't put up *your* flag! You were our e-ne-*mee!*' And they say, '*Yes,* we are being liberated *too!*' And we have a big *fight* right there. Everybody pulling down flags—" He laughed and coughed. "—fighting, laughing, all the same time! Tearing up the flags! But I come to my beautiful Paris and it is not amusing." He pointed with his thumb.

Ross got out his cigarettes and gave Claude one. Claude took deep puffs and continued to talk, "I came back, and they caught me with a box of American cigarette, and fine me for making traffic. The agent, he didn't take me to the Commissariat. He just fine me *right there in the street!* O.K., I pay the fine, then I say, 'O.K., you have to do these things because they are your job, and like that. Now we can talk like two men.' And I say, 'Why you fine me? An American boy gave me a whole box of cigarette because I took him in the P.T.T. to buy one of each kind of postage stamps.' I say, 'You know who is making traffic with cigarette, *chocolat,* all kinds of clothes and like that. And you don't do any-*thing!*" Then he gave me back my box of cigarette." He pointed behind with his thumb. "Government!"

Finally after a turn in the road, down a long hill, they saw a network of pale lights spread out over a wide valley. "That's Paris," Claude said. "Why you have your big bag?"

"They're sending me to school."

"Why the army send you to school? The war is finish."

"*Vraiment,* the war is finished," Ross shrugged. And anything it might have accomplished would seem to have faded away. All things were sliding neatly back into their old places, all except one. He had grasped that one thing, and he was trying to hold on; yet he had no clear idea what it was.

The long dingy streets of the north of Paris brightened a bit as they moved toward the center of town. Finally Claude turned into the curb and parked. The street was full of soldiers.

*"Terminus!"* Claude shouted. *"Terminus!* Boulevard Haussmann!"

# XV

Monsieur and Madame Bercy, and Hébert were the first to get out. They collected themselves and fled, while the rest remained to shake hands with Ross. Monsieur de Bonfons was first to offer his hand, "As we have been saying, monsieur, we like your great willingness to help. That is the American spirit. And I think in France you will find that people are only the better friends after an argument."

Mademoiselle Flaunet shook his hand quickly, *"Voilà,* Monsieur de Bonfons, precisely my sentiments." Thérèse waved bye-bye American style.

As they disappeared along the boulevard into the crowds, Claude raised his fist after them, "Monday morning! Be on time!"

They were parked in front of the Hotel Ambassador, which was an officers' barracks for the American army, so Ross decided to go there to make the phone call. Halfway across the sidewalk a man stepped in front of him. "A moment, monsieur," he whispered. "You will sell me gasoline?"

Ross elbowed him aside and went into the lobby to the

desk clerk who sat reading a comic book and chewing gum.

"I want an ambulance," Ross told him.

He went on reading while he plugged in his switchboard, announced a number to the operator, and handed Ross his headphone. There was already a voice on the wire.

"I'm at the Ambassador Hotel," Ross said. "I want an ambulance."

The voice repeated the name of the hotel and hung up. Ross walked back out to the street where Claude asked him, "What they tell you to do?"

"It's all right. We just wait."

Leaning against the weapons-carrier, Ross noticed an ambulance trying to turn into the block. A lieutenant stepped out and headed toward the hotel, carrying a medical bag. It had not been three minutes since Ross made the call. As Ross walked toward him, the lieutenant asked, "You call for an ambulance?"

"Have your driver follow us, sir," Ross asked him. "It's about forty kilometers."

The lieutenant turned and walked back toward the ambulance. "That's quite a ways," he said. And on some intuition he asked Ross, "Is it an American soldier?"

"It's—she works for the army. Bad accident on the road," Ross told him.

"Well, kid, you know what this town is like on a Friday night. We have to keep this buggy on call."

"But she fell under our weapons-carrier, Lieutenant. And the wheel went over her. She's a United States army employee."

"American woman?"

"French."

The lieutenant sat down on the seat beside his driver and thought a moment. Then he said, "That your weapons-carrier?"

With relief, Ross said, "Yes sir, Lieutenant."

"Then I don't see why you drove all the way in here for an ambulance." He motioned to his driver to go on. "Why don't you bring her in, yourself?"

Claude said, "But the way she scream. She is broken inside."

"Let's find a police station," Ross told him.

Ross got in and Claude gunned away from the curb and turned at the corner. Two blocks on, he slammed into a parking space and pointed out the window. "Over there, the Opera. Under the front steps in the Commissariat de Police."

As Ross walked in, one of the policemen behind the counter motioned him forward, *"C'est pourquoi, monsieur?"*

"We had an accident on the road, forty kilometers from here. A woman was hurt badly—a French woman. We need a doctor and an ambulance."

The policeman smiled, "We will see what is possible. Take a seat and we will see."

Ross took a seat on a long bench against the wall. When he was called back to the counter, the policeman smiled again, "There is not an ambulance in the city with the capacity to go the forty kilometers and return, monsieur. That is eighty kilometers. We have no gasoline—only synthetics—but you, monsieur, can't you get an American truck?"

Ross told him he had one, and went back out in front of the Opera to find Claude. The Opera was the first building in Paris that he recognized from his college professor's post cards.

"What the *flic* tell you?" Claude asked him.

He didn't answer. He just climbed into the weapons-carrier.

Claude drove around the square and headed back out of the city.

When they were on the road, Ross said, "Thanks, Claude."

"Ah, *non, pourquoi* thanks?"

"For Madame Bernard."

Claude was silent. Then he said, "You forget about this, *heh?* You don't understand anything, so you forget about it. You think nobody help her but that little *mignonne,* because they make traffic with the German? Ah, *non!*"

"You mean Yvette was a collaborationist too?" Ross asked him.

"That is not *the* reason," Claude said.

"Then what's happening?" Ross asked him.

"You are an American boy, so you don't know. You never was tired in your life. Now me, I never was tired, because I was always doing the things the German did not want me to do!" He laughed. "When I was a prisoner they let us starve a couple of week, and then they say, 'Volunteer to work in the factory and you can eat. Lot of your friends do that. Don't you want to volunteer, too?' So we all volunteer. And there was a lot of German girl working in the factory, and we see them, boy! We didn't touch a woman for a long time! Then one of these girl served the food to us, she is looking at me every time I come in the line. And I look at her. And sometimes she gave me one extra piece of bread under the dish, so I got a piece of aluminum and I made her a little ring and give it under the dish, too. But we cannot be together. But we watch, watch, and one night I make excuse to go stand by the kitchen and she is coming out, and we have a kiss. Then we both run away quick. The German began to look for that piece of aluminum, and they ask her how she got it and beat her up. They give her six month, and give me three month in the dark. And every third day was my good day, when I could walk out in the light and eat. But that didn't do anything to me. And when I was coming back from the prison to the camp, I was on the same train with all those same girls going to work in the morning, and they ask the guard, 'What that nice French boy was doing to be in prison?' And the guard say, 'He was having a love with a German girl.' And then they say, 'Oh, such a *nice* boy, it is too bad.' And I am just looking out the window of the train, and I smile. But a man has to do something like that, all the time, or he will get very tired, like—" he pointed behind with his thumb.

Ross thought of his college French professor and wondered what he could possibly have understood about the

French, and they about him. He had made his students work to learn the language, with the promise that here a black man could survive, or simply avoid being black, which was it? No one in the class had ever thought to ask that question. Ross had a growing awareness at the back of his mind that here he was no one at all—or no one in particular, as though there was no Paul Ross any more. On beyond desegregation—is that what it would be? It was not that here he had brought nothing of himself with him, only that here no one had any idea what he had lived through, any more than he could understand what had happened here, even when they talked about it, as he might talk about a black child being a Cub Scout in America. Too much would be lost putting it into words, so long after being that child. And was it any longer important? Here, it would be no more important to anyone else than what had happened to Claude, or to Madame Bernard. For the others in the weapons-carrier who had fled into the night in the streets of Paris, Madame Bernard had been hated, feared, then crushed under the weight of their own bodies. An accident had only speeded a process between them already begun, which had a familiar logic, described to him as the method of pigs in the winter, when the ground is cold. How had Skin said it? ". . . Come a time when it's too cold to be wallering in the mud, they all up together and put one down where they can all sit on him, and from then on that's the nigger in the bunch." But as Skin had explained it, the nigger is chosen not for his weakness, but for his strength; yet Madame Bernard appeared frail, old, and alcoholic. For which reason, was there no meaning or logic in what had happened?

When they were back at the sanitarium and drove through the gate, Yvette ran out to meet them. Ross called to her, "Is she O.K.?"

Yvette was happy and smiling, "Oh, the doctor gave her the needle. She has no pain."

"*What* doctor?"

"Your army sent one," she said, delighted with the way

it was all turning out. "He came just right after you left, and said he was sent by that place you talked on the telephone."

"And he *left* her here?"

"He had only a jeep. He said it was very serious, to wait and go in the ambulance from Paris." Then she asked cautiously, "You did not get an ambulance?"

Ross climbed out and faced her, "No, Yvette. No." Yvette held her breath while he told her that the American ambulance refused to come and the French had no gasoline. When her breath came back to her, her arms went around his neck and held on to him, not as before when she was angered by the others and made a show of kissing him. He put his arm around the heavy metal harness she wore, "We can borrow what we need to make her warm and comfortable. Don't worry, Yvette, we can get her there."

As they went inside, she said helplessly, "I wish you could know how important it is that you do this for Madame Bernard, but I cannot tell you. No one else will help her—"

"There is nothing you need to tell me," he said to her and refused to hear any more. He and Claude asked permission to borrow two mattresses from the sanitarium, and laid one on top of the other on the floor of the weapons-carrier, and they borrowed blankets and a pillow. Then they went to Madame Bernard. Her head was bandaged, and a bandage was wrapped firmly around her ribs, another around her wrist.

Ross asked Yvette, "Has she any family in Paris?"

"No, no one," she said. "We live together in Montmartre. We adopted each other after—"

Yvette would not finish, but Madame Bernard continued, "There is no one at Paris now. My husband was killed near the end of the war. They thought he was the Blue Canary."

Yvette gasped and attempted to silence Madame Bernard.

Madame Bernard smiled at her, "It is no longer important. You know what that means, *the Blue Canary?*" she asked Ross. He shook his head, no. "The Nazis did not know either," she said to him. "They thought the Blue Canary was a man, but it was a woman."

"Madame Bernard!" Yvette pleaded.

"It is no longer important," she told Yvette firmly, and then to Ross, "You know Metz?"

"Metz?" he asked.

"Your 5th and 95th Divisions came there. In the city was a fat little man named Anton Dunkern as the ss brigade fuehrer. He was also ss leader for all of Lorraine, but he was no ss combat general, only a fat little party official. We showed your 5th Division where to strike his artillery positions."

"*Madame Bernard!*" Yvette bellowed at her.

"Poor Yvette," Madame Bernard said to Ross. "Now she must know," she said sadly. "It is no longer important, not to anyone, not even to ourselves, Yvette."

Yvette began to cry and hid her face against Ross as Madame Bernard continued, "I was a child in Metz. It was a long time ago. It is difficult to explain, we were under Kaiser Wilhelm der Zweite, but since the war of fourteen, Metz again was France. You will give me an American cigarette?"

Ross gave her a cigarette and lighted it for her. "Now I remember like yesterday," she continued, "how the *dienstmädchen*—the maid—she used to take me and my little brother for walks in the springtime near the Kaserne. That's the place in the square where all the soldiers live. There would be music from the military orchestra, and the soldiers would throw down from the windows pieces of *zweiback* for us children, with notes tied around for the *dienstmädchen.* Even once the Kaiser himself came to us —and there were black, white, and red ribbons all around the Square. His arm was too short to touch his hat, so he saluted to us children with a gold rod with a small gold hand at the end of it." She attempted to demonstrate but felt a sudden pain. She seemed frightened for a moment, then went on talking, "And at Christmas there would be coming—" Again pain was written in her eyes. After a silence, she said, "And now I am made tired enough to sleep, while you do what you plan to do." She handed Ross her cigarette and closed her eyes.

Yvette buttoned Madame Bernard's coat, then wrapped her in a blanket. Ross and Claude, and the old woman helping, lifted her from the table, while Yvette guided them through the door and down the steps to the mattresses on the floor of the weapons-carrier.

Ross went back for his duffel bag; then he and Yvette climbed in and watched over her while Claude drove slowly along the road to Paris.

With some relief, Yvette whispered, "I am sure she is asleep—she learned how to do that." Then she added, with almost a smile, "When she slept, we all knew to fear nothing!"

"I would never have thought—" Ross began.

"Oh, I was a joke, monsieur," she said drolly. "I caught polio in the Resistance—there was no way they could get rid of me!"

"How did they take care of you?"

"Among us were many good doctors."

"So after that—you learned judo?"

She laughed, "Some of it. There was nothing else they knew how to teach me. I wanted to go to Portugal to be warm and to swim, but there was never a time."

They were cold. Ross opened his duffel bag and took out his blankets, one for Madame Bernard and the other for Yvette. Yvette insisted that they share it. She sat close to him with her head on his shoulder, and took his hand. "I don't even know your name, monsieur," she said mock disapprovingly.

"Ross," he said, looking away from her, having mistaken her tone in the darkness.

Yvette turned his face toward hers. "*What* Ross?" she whispered.

"Paul."

"Paul," she said softly, and kissed him.

It was hard for him to imagine Yvette liking him. "You

don't owe me anything," he said.

"Ooooh," she said, poking fun at him, "then you can't be unhappy to kiss me," and waited for him to do so.

He kissed her, then put his arms around her.

"You do not mind my bird cage? My brace?"

"No, I don't mind your bird cage," he said, and his hand found the metal frame and caressed it.

"It is not for always," she said. "I can come out of it and fly around whenever I want to."

"Don't fly away," he said.

"No," she assured him, then yawned and burrowed within his embrace, and closed her eyes.

Through the night they took turns keeping a close watch on Madame Bernard as one drowsed in the other's arms, and they struggled against falling asleep both at the same time by kissing each other. By the first glow of morning they reached the dew-covered streets of the north of Paris. There they took on an escort of working men on bicycles, and once they were out-distanced by a convoy of American army jeeps, command cars, and trucks loaded with helmeted, yawning men. The entourage peddled doggedly on, the weapons-carrier leading the way.

They placed Madame Bernard in the Lariboisière. Ross had orders to report to the American House at Cité Universitaire, far to the south of Paris, on Monday morning. Yvette shared an apartment with Madame Bernard in Montmartre, within walking distance of the hospital, and she invited Ross to stay the weekend.

# *XVI*

ON THE following Friday, Madame Bernard died. Yvette gave the details and funeral arrangements to the newspapers, to which they added what further information they had.

*Le Figaro* reported: *To the Gestapo, and to the Allied Forces, she was known only by her nom de guerre, the "Blue Canary." In November 1944, when it was evident to everyone that Germany was losing the war, Radio Berlin triumphantly made the announcement that the Canary had been captured, and executed by manual strangulation, in Metz.*

*At that time, all contact with this agent within the Resistance was lost, and the German report was assumed to be true.*

*Paris-Soir* printed a statement of condolence from Charles de Gaulle, and editorialized: *Since the war, for various reasons with respect to continuing activities of the Resistance, habitual secrecy remains. German war criminals are being sought from country to country, and for this certain French collaborationists are being watched, rather than taken; thus the valiant and tragic history of this agent cannot be revealed. Other agents, like the rest of the French people, are busy pulling together the threads of their previous lives, or merely trying to find means of making a living, in which process, what they have done and been during the war is of considerably minor importance, except in the case of some of those master printers and engravers who supplied the Underground, and the Allies, with copies, properly signed and authorized, of official German documents and passports, who are now—somewhat reluctantly—manufacturing their own private supply of the banknotes of France.*

At the cemetery, during the simple ceremony Ross stood at attention holding the French flag beside Yvette and the rabbi. Yvette held a machine gun. It was a broken machine gun, else it would have been confiscated by the police. About forty people attended, nameless members of the Resistance in Paris.

As they turned to leave, Paul recognized Monsieur de Bonfons and Monsieur Bercy. With enormous grief, Monsieur de Bonfons extended his hand to Yvette, "A most, most unfortunate circumstance."

Monsieur Bercy, who was in tears, also extended his hand, "If we could only have reached an army doctor, she would be alive," he said.

"But we did," Ross told him. "An army doctor came just after everyone left."

Monsieur de Bonfons put his hand on Ross' shoulder, "For the failure of the telephone, no one can blame you."

"The telephone went dead, but someone heard enough to know, or trace the call," Ross told him. "An army doctor came just after everyone left to come here."

"And he *refused* to take her?" de Bonfons asked.

"She decided to wait for the ambulance from Paris, but I was unable to get one," Ross said.

De Bonfons was furious, "You would let a woman in her condition decide for herself? You would also let a woman in her condition not go to the army where they could have saved her?"

"I was not with her when the doctor came," Ross explained.

"And why were you not with her? Were you not the one who asked to be in charge of her?"

"But I had come here to Paris, with you—and the others."

Monsieur de Bonfons drew away from him, "You would accuse me—?"

"No, monsieur. No one knew—"

De Bonfons began to scream, "*—and you did not go back to that miserable sanitarium where you left her?*"

Without words, Yvette began to scream at Bercy and de Bonfons, wildly flinging handfuls of earth from the grave in their faces. Some of the members of the Resistance understood that they were to join in with Yvette, and were beginning to do so when Ross, holding the flag pole, raised it as if to throw it at their heads. In that moment, one could have imagined him a prophet, like Jonah and Jason, bringing the word. In their confusion, they became silent waiting for him to explain.

He stood trembling and speechless, but when finally he spoke, his voice was angry and firm, *"C'est une histoire de cochons,"* he began. "This is a story of pigs. When it is winter, and too cold for pigs to live in the mud, they conspire to select one among them to sit upon. It goes without saying, this one is selected like a slave, not for his weakness but for his strength, to bear the burdens of the rest. . . ."

*"Vraiment, c'est une histoire de cochons,"* he continued. . . .